Carly & Otis

Show The World

Matthew Beggarly

DEDICATION

To my beautiful, amazing daughter, Lindsay Beggarly,
I never got to read you a story, and it is something
that I truly regret.
I hope that one day you will read this book to my
grandchildren.
Your amazing spirit and beautiful soul are the
inspiration for Carly.
Thank you for being in my life. I love you, Kiddo.

"Remember, if you have to compromise your
principles to be accepted, you are being accepted by
the wrong people."

~Me

Preface

The story of Carly and Otis came to me late one night as I was sitting on the bow of the LeBateu while sailing The Great Loop of North America.

It was well past midnight on a dark, moonless night in a secluded, sheltered waterway in early April 2017. As I sat all alone dangling my legs over the side of the ship, a group of dolphins swam nearby.

I happened to have a flashlight with me, so I started playing flashlight tag with the dolphins. I shined the light onto the water, and they swam to it; and then I moved the light to another spot on the water, and they swam to it again. Our game went on for almost an hour, and I think I had almost as much fun as they did.

It was in this magical moment under the stars when I realized that like grains of sand on a beach, each of us is just one small part of the world around us. And yet, as mere grains of sand, we have the greatest impact on our world. We hold in our hands the end of this world, not for just ourselves, but for every living organism on this planet. Every choice we make influences everything around us. We are the rulers of our own domains, and each of us has power over creation and destruction.

Although we may be rulers of our environment, a ruler needs to know when to stop and listen to the creatures, nature, and all that make up the only home we have—planet Earth. They need us just as much as we need them. This is what Carly and Otis is about. It is about learning that we all are one with everything. And if we simply listen, we may discover that perhaps we are not rulers after all, but just grains of sand.

CARLY & OTIS

Table of Contents

ACKNOWLEDGMENTS

First and foremost, there are no words adequate enough to express my deepest appreciation to the young woman whose quick action in the restaurant saved my life on that fateful day. Without your willingness to help a stranger, I certainly would not be here today to tell my stories. You are my hero, and I will be eternally grateful to you.

Thank you to all of my family and friends who have supported my dreams along the way.

Thank you Mary Replogle, my editor and friend, for molding my raw materials into readable tales.

And thank you Bryn Winebrunner for your delightful, original artwork for the cover.

࿔ ✳ ࿔

CHAPTER 1

THAR SHE BLOWS

It was a Wednesday in January on the Intracoastal Pass near the Devil's Gate in Georgia when she spotted the whale.

Carly, just 23 years old and already a seasoned marine biologist from the University of Miami, was the first to spot the magnificent creature. She yelled like Captain Ahab, "Thar she blows!" from the bow of the Mother Earth, a 100-foot-long, marine-life research vessel, which had been granted special permission to sail close enough to study and tag the remaining North Atlantic right whales.

Considering that the North Atlantic right whale is now nearly extinct, this would be a somber yet exciting experience for anyone, especially for a scientist whose vocation is to study the majesty of earth's largest and gentlest animals. The opportunity to get close to any of these remaining 35 right whales is an opportunity that no self-respecting marine biologist could pass up. And blonde-haired, blue-eyed Carly, with her infectious smile and hopefulness for the world, had eagerly signed up to be part of this adventure.

Carly's father had been a commercial fisherman from the waterfront town of Burlington, Georgia, who had been exposed to all forms of sea life. So, naturally, Carly grew up near the water and has always felt at home around marine life. Too many people get caught up in the rush of the world; however, the sea provided the tranquility Carly loved. It was her understanding of mankind's origins that drew her into being one with nature. The sea holds a special place for her, and living near America's Intracoastal region all of her life made this a perfect fit.

The area called Devil's Gate is difficult to navigate. The water can go from shallow to even shallower on a moment's notice. Then the water will suddenly become extremely deep with a vicious series of currents that can make running aground and becoming stranded a common occurrence.

The shallow and deep-water areas are what draw marine life to this area. For dolphins, manatees, and several forms of whales, this is the ideal setting in which to give birth. Protected from the predators of the ocean, this area not only provides time for the animals to give birth, but also time to teach their young as they travel south to warmer waters.

The Intracoastal consists of patches of land and marshes that are intermingled with permanent waterways, and wildlife thrives here. There are alligators, birds, wild boar, horses, turtles, deer, snakes, insects, and hundreds of different species of fish, which makes feeding easy for newborn marine mammals. The Intracoastal is the largest expanse of open wildlife in the United States, and it is the gateway to the expanse of the world's oceans.

Being a child of the sea herself, Carly had always loved the variety of wildlife that comes to this area. She was raised to respect the water and the life it brings to all. Carly can recall each of her connections to the creatures that dwell in the sea—even back to when she was nine years old.

There was the leatherback sea turtle she saved from her father's nets and the family of dolphins she swam with every season as they traveled through the area where Carly grew up. There always seemed to be an experience of almost being able to communicate with them.

When Carly was just 16 years old, she witnessed a horror that she will never forget. While out with her father on one of their deep-sea fishing excursions, they came across a beached whale. A magnificent right whale had beached itself on the sand of a very popular tourist beach on Jekyll Island and was unable to sustain its life. It was in that moment that Carly became determined to find out the reason why whales beach themselves; it was that tragedy that set her future in stone. Carly was going to become a marine biologist specializing in whale research.

As Carly stood on the bow of the research vessel, she thought back to the sight of that dying whale, and a tear came to her eye as she took in the beauty of seeing a new one swimming through the water with ease. Within moments the Mother Earth was near the creature, and just as the whale surfaced, Carly and the whale made eye contact.

Suddenly, Carly felt an inexplicable pain, almost

to her core, and a shudder of fear and anxiousness came over her. She yelled through her headset to stop the ship, crying out, "*Stop! Stop! Stop!*"

The captain of the Mother Earth shifted the engines into full reverse, which brought the ship to a rumbling halt.

Then fellow biologist John came running to meet Carly on the deck. "What? What? We're not close enough!" he exclaimed.

Carly explained that the whale was pregnant and in pain. Carly did not know how or why she knew this, but she just knew it. It is often said that the eyes are the windows to the soul, so perhaps making eye contact with the whale is what gave Carly this amazing insight.

As the rest of the crew of 10 came rushing to find out what was happening and to see the great whale, things seemed to speed up drastically.

Now it is common knowledge that one does not get near a birthing whale because, just as in any birth, it is a painful experience. Even for a creature the size of a whale, giving birth to another whale surely must be tremendously painful. So, for this reason, it is dangerous to try to get close.

Throwing caution to the wind, Carly demanded that her dive equipment be brought to her and that the launch be lowered.

"Are you nuts? No way are you going in there!" John exclaimed.

"Try and stop me!" Carly replied.

John relented and gave the crew their instructions, and then he and Carly climbed into the launch. Within a few minutes, they were near the whale.

Carly quickly checked her gear and then kicked

back over the edge of the boat and into the cool, cloudy, brisk waters of the Intracoastal. As she drew near to the beautiful whale, she could hear the sounds of a whale song. Although Carly knew better than to get close to the whale, she could not resist. She swam right up to the eyes of the gigantic whale and looked deeply into them.

Carly saw an overwhelming sadness in the whale's eyes. It was a sadness that she had seen only from a distance before. Now she could see it up close and deeply. Carly knew immediately that this whale—and all whales—carried a sadness deep inside them.

As they were staring into each other's eyes, the water around Carly turned bloody, and the whale song turned into violent, painful squeals. Instinctively, Carly looked toward the hind section of the whale just in time to see the beginning of a new life spring from its mother.

Carly gasped and almost sucked in some water as she watched this beautiful and most natural experience. Before her very eyes, Carly witnessed the birth of Number 36. A clumsy, giant mass of flesh emerged from the mother and instantly looked in Carly's direction. And at the same time, the mother whale started to turn and move, actually being mindful of Carly's presence.

Carly looked up towards the surface and saw the bottom of the launch where John was waiting. But then to her horror, she also saw the bottom of another small craft about 30 yards away. She knew what it was and immediately headed for the surface with determination in her every kick.

Just as she broke the surface of the water, Carly heard John yelling, "*Get away! Get away!*"

Carly's worst fear became a reality. Someone in a small speedboat had seen the whale and broke every law of protection just to fulfill a selfish desire to boast that he saw a whale.

As John pulled Carly into the launch, Carly began frantically waving off the craft as she shed her gear. Then Carly saw the name on the weekender vessel; it was the Otis Day. Finally, the boat withdrew as a result of Carly and John's protests, and the whales began to surface.

The mother whale was the first to appear, surfacing slowly and surveying her surroundings. Coming within just a few feet of the launch, she made eye contact with Carly again. This eye contact seemed to convey a simple message of gratitude to Carly for being with her during the birth of her baby. And soon the newborn whale made its first appearance at the surface, too, right next to its mother. And Carly exclaimed, "Otis! Thar you blow!"

CHAPTER 2

NUMBER 36

As the newly named whale and its mother swam off through the Intracoastal Waterway, Carly and John were awestruck by what they had just witnessed.

Most whale births have been documented only in captivity. And as far as Carly and John knew, they were the first persons to have witnessed a whale birth in the whale's natural habitat. Carly could not contain her emotions as Number 36, Otis, swam away, and she began sobbing openly. John did not know what to do, except to wonder if the heavy blood trail following the whales was normal.

Towering at 6 feet 6 inches tall, 42-year-old John was built like a long-distance runner. With an unruly beard and a head of hair that rivaled Einstein's, he was the epitome of what one would imagine a maritime explorer to look like.

As the team leader, John never intimidated his team. He always inspired them to think for themselves and allowed them to make their own judgment calls. And in Carly's case, it paid off.

As they were returning to Mother Earth, John pointed to the blood trail and asked Carly for her opinion about it. Carly slowly regained her composure and replied in a slow, controlled voice, "John, something is wrong. I don't know if that blood trail is normal or not, but we need to follow them. I heard it in her song. I felt her pain, and I saw it in her eyes."

John nodded in agreement.

Once back aboard Mother Earth, John asked the captain to follow the blood trail and to keep a safe distance from the whales. Knowing that the low-spot shallows would not hinder the Mother Earth's ability to follow them, the captain readily complied.

Carly stood on the bow of the boat, and with her binoculars kept a watchful eye on the pair of whales. As the sun slowly touched the horizon, the crew brought lights onto the deck to spotlight the water while the sonar technicians monitored the whales' trail. The Intracoastal is a tricky seaway. Patches of land and narrow passes weaving between the barrier islands make it a difficult and hazardous route.

As night approached, the tides went out, and the whales settled into a large area of deep water that opens to the Atlantic Ocean. These basins are usually created where several waterways meet, and they are perfect areas for such majestic animals to rest. Carly could not sleep, so she went to the sonar room to watch Mama and Otis, Number 36, on the sonar.

However, Carly soon began to doze off. As she slept, she relived Otis' birth over and over again in her dreams. The pain she felt for the mother and the immediate connection she felt to Otis as their eyes met made Carly very restless. She stirred and twitched as images of the bleeding mother whale flashed through her dreams, and she felt the mother whale's intense pain. What had started as a beautiful dream turned into a nightmare as images of the beached whale from her childhood caused Carly to awaken with a scream.

Everyone in the sonar room jumped to their feet. John ran to Carly, placed his strong hand on her shoulder, and insisted that she go to her cabin. Carly returned to her cabin and instantly fell asleep. This time there were no nightmares, just peace and quiet.

As the sun rose on the horizon the next morning, Carly was already on the deck. On her way topside, she had stopped in the sonar room to confirm that the two whales were still out there.

Carly was very familiar with this area of the Intracoastal—100 miles from the shores where she grew up, yet so close to the open ocean. Carly knew that if the mother whale did not stop bleeding soon, predators would be upon them. The ocean can be unforgiving, and Carly knew this very well.

As the tides came in, the Mama and Otis continued their journey. This time they headed toward Jekyll Island—that same island where, as a child, Carly had seen her first and only beached whale. The idea of the mother heading there was a somber reminder of what can happen.

But this is why Carly had become a marine biologist. She believed that the meaning of her life was to discover why whales beach themselves. Carly quietly prayed to not learn why today.

As the ship tracked the whales, the blood trail continued, and everyone knew that this was not good.

John approached Carly, and the look in her eyes confirmed that this was a dire situation. There was too much blood in the water, and sharks would arrive soon to investigate. Whales have very few natural predators, and sharks are one of them. Sharks can usually get in a bite or two, but to Number 36 that could be deadly. After all, Otis was just one day old.

Before long and about 15 miles from Jekyll Island, Carly saw her first sign of sharks—a dorsal fin had appeared near the whales. And soon there were more. It was rare to see a shark in the Intracoastal; however, it was not totally unheard of in the deep-water areas like where they were now.

Carly started crying again because she knew what was about to happen. John saw the dorsal fins, too, and stood beside Carly. He told her that the sonar had reported that the mother was shifting her position and heading toward Jekyll Island and shallower waters. Sharks big enough to take on a whale do not like shallow water since it limits their ability to strike. Carly knew this, but she also knew that it limited the mother's ability to maneuver as well.

The mother surfaced close to the boat and looked directly at Carly as if knowing that Carly was her guardian. However, the look she gave Carly this time was full of emotion. It was a look that only a few people can read, and it conveyed a range of emotions—fear, pain, longing, understanding, panic, and also a plea for help. The mother whale's cries were now extremely loud and could be heard above the water for the first time.

Mama and Otis stayed close to Mother Earth. But eventually, more and more dorsal fins began appearing.

Mama moved away from the ship, but Otis stayed close to Mother Earth as if it was now somehow protecting him while his mother swam off to divert the predators' attention.

Mama swam as deeply as she could in the 80 feet of water. Then she saw the first large shark dart towards her. She maneuvered her body and fins to slap that shark away as another came toward her from the other side.

The second shark got passed Mama's defenses and took an opportunistic bite from her side. The pain must have been excruciating, despite its small size compared to Mama's size.

Then another shark appeared, and then another, and before long several smaller sharks had also joined in the fray. But Mama refused to surface. She stayed where she had the advantage of deep water so that she could maneuver and defend herself. Mama fought hard. Her job was to protect Number 36, and she was going to do just that!

As the sharks started their frenzy, Mama used her fins and tail to keep them at a distance; but every now and again, one would get through and bite her. Mama eventually grew tired and needed to surface.

As Mama surfaced off the port side of the Mother Earth, Carly caught her gaze. And this time Mama was pleading, "He is yours. Please take care of him."

Carly felt this message, so she stayed close to the starboard side with Otis, telling him, "Stay close, baby. Mama is going to be fine."

Mama found herself in the fight of her life, and the entire crew witnessed it firsthand. Before long the ship's crew saw a giant dorsal fin heading towards Mama. Mama also saw it and swam toward the

11

surface, this time with more vigor. Just as she reached the surface, almost full body out of the water, Mama saw her attacker, a huge tiger shark. She had timed her surface break perfectly, and she came crashing down on the mega predator.

Just as Mama crashed, the shark must have realized that its end was near, and it took a huge bite out of Mama as she took the life out of it.

Being opportunists, the other sharks turned their attention away from Mama and now focused on the sinking carcass of the huge shark. Mama made a break towards Jekyll Island as fast as she could with Mother Earth and Otis trailing closely behind.

Now bleeding from both inside and outside, Mama was screaming in her songs. It was not like any whale song anyone had ever heard. And as Mother Earth rounded the tip of Jekyll Island, Carly saw her nightmare again. At about the same place where Carly had seen the first beached whale, she now saw a wounded and bleeding Mama flipping up onto the beach.

When Carly encountered that beached whale so many years ago, she had not seen how it had struggled to get its tremendous mass onto the beach. However, this time she helplessly watched Mama's struggle. She saw Mama's struggle to rest, and she saw a horror that she had hoped to never see again.

Carly looked over the stern at Otis and her only thought was, "My God! He was Number 36, and now he has become Number 35...all in the span of just one day." Tears streamed down Carly's face as a frightened Otis, now Number 35, looked up at her.

CHAPTER 3

MOTHER EARTH

As the Mother Earth approached the beach, the scene was turning hectic. Tourists were running and screaming as the nearly 80-ton sea creature came ashore, bleeding and thrashing about on the sand. People were running to Mama, vehicles hurried down the beach to see what was happening, and lights were flashing all over the place. John ordered the crew to prepare the launch again.

Carly, John, and a few others boarded the launch, which was then lowered into the water. Almost immediately, Otis came alongside. Carly could not fully understand why Otis was not trying to get to his mother yet. It seemed almost as if his mother had told him to stay by Carly; but, of course, whales can't talk. Or can they?

As the launch landed in the waves, it was full speed ahead towards the beach on Jekyll Island. And as soon as they got close enough, Carly and John leapt into the sea and ran as fast as they could through the waves to the shore.

John waved away the onlookers and talked with the emergency personnel who had already arrived on the scene. While John handled the crowd, Carly ran straight to Mama's head and looked her in the eye for the fourth time in a single day. Then Carly placed her hands on the whale and laid her head on her and wept as she felt Mama struggling to breathe.

Her valiant fight saved her baby, but had cost Mama her life. And Carly knew it. Carly tried to soothe Mama and reassure her that her new baby was all right. "He is safe. He is safe." Carly repeated.

As Carly looked into the mother whale's eyes, she again felt the connection that each somehow understood what the other was thinking. And as she looked into Carly's eyes, Mama knew that what Carly was saying was true—that her new baby was safe. And deep down in her soul, Carly felt a calling that she was now Otis' mother.

Carly stayed with Mama for hours, crying. She never left the side of the beautiful animal. As the day came to an end at sunset, Mama passed from this life into the next. And with Mama's passing, Carly's connection with her also passed.

It was only then that Carly finally stirred. John startled her when he approached, "Carly, it is done."

Carly needed to see Otis. She needed to see her new baby. She left John standing on the beach as she walked back into the ocean. And to her delight, she did not have to go far. Otis came to the surface not more than 20 yards out.

At that moment, Carly felt a strong feeling of love as waves of happiness and understanding swept over her. As she gazed at Otis, Carly could not help but feel a connection to him and an understanding of what he was thinking.

Eventually, the launch pulled alongside Carly, and John pulled her aboard. Carly could not speak; all she could do was look at Otis.

Knowing his crew very well, John sensed that something special was going on, and he turned the launch in Otis' direction. As they neared the majestic baby, Carly jumped into the water and swam to him.

John nearly turned white with fear. This was now a wild animal without its mother, and the night sky was getting very dark. John had no idea what to expect; but as Carly touched Otis, it became clear that all would be fine. Carly and Otis had a connection.

It is well known that animals communicate with each other within their own species and that they can learn to take direction from humans. However, some also believe that communication between two different species is possible. Is this "communication" merely speculation of how people imagine an animal might respond? Or is there actual communication?

Since whales have the largest brains of any animal, why should they not be capable of communicating with us? It is just a question of whether we can understand them.

In the case of Carly and Otis, it was like they could read each other's minds. Otis was not afraid. He was comfortable being with the woman who witnessed his birth. However, Carly could tell he was sad and that he missed his mother.

It was during this exchange that Mother Earth drew near, and a crew member started shouting for Carly to board the launch and return to the ship.

It sounded urgent, so Carly patted Otis one last time as she pulled herself onto the launch.

Once aboard the research vessel, a crew member reported to Carly and John that the sonar readings showed several massive forms heading their way.

John went to the sonar room to confirm the readings as Carly stood on the bow with her baby Otis by the side of the ship.

A few minutes later, John returned and told Carly that approximately twelve other right whales were heading towards them; and shortly thereafter, they spotted the first one on the surface—then another, and then another. Before long there were about a dozen of the remaining right whales surrounding Mother Earth.

They believed that this phenomenon had never been witnessed before because so little was actually known about these creatures. Carly could not help but wonder if these other whales had heard Mama's cries and had come to help; but now, sadly, to mourn.

Although exhausted and worn, Carly could not leave the bow of the ship. She and John were fascinated by what they saw—whales coming so close to Mother Earth as if they were treating it as one of their own.

Several came alongside, and Carly made eye contact with these whales as well. It was as if each one was thanking her and then meeting the newest member of their kind.

Otis did not move away from Mother Earth's side. He remained cautious to not leave the protection of his new mother despite the presence of the others of his kind, and Carly felt a sense of peace in his being there.

As the moonlight danced on the sea all around the Mother Earth, the whales remained at the surface watching Mama whose body was still on the beach.

"It seems like they are paying their respects. You know...like how elephants mourn their dead. These whales seem to be mourning Otis' mother," John said.

"Has this ever happened before," Carly asked with a cracking voice.

"I don't think so. But I don't believe that anyone has ever looked toward the sea during a beaching to know if it has," John replied.

Carly looked at John and wanted to say something, but hesitated. John could see it in her expression and asked, "What is it?"

Carly said softly, "This may sound crazy—and I mean really crazy—but I think I understand what both Mama and Otis are thinking."

Stunned by what Carly had just said, John replied, "No. That is impossible. There is no way for that to happen. You are just attributing expected human responses to the whales. It is called anthropomorphism, Carly, and it is our way of connecting with animals. This has been a very emotional 24 hours, and this is just a natural way for you to process it all."

"No! It is more than that! You'll see!" Carly responded a bit harshly.

Carly was exhausted. The last 24 hours had been very difficult and she needed to rest. She looked over the bow towards the water and blew a kiss to Otis who was still at the side of of Mother Earth.

As Carly walked to her cabin, she wondered if John was right. "Maybe I *am* just projecting my own desires onto this situation," she pondered.

No. She knew this was different. After all of her studying, she knew that whale brains were enormous and that whales have inhabited this planet much longer than the human race.

As she dozed off, Carly thought that maybe, just maybe, they had been talking to us all along, but we just did not know how to hear them. Maybe the stress of the last 24 hours allowed her to finally listen—and to hear. And that thought comforted her as she drifted off into a deep, restful slumber.

With the dawning of a new day and some clarity of her feelings, Carly ran topside to see Otis and to find out if the other whales were still nearby. Surely enough, as the sun peeked over the horizon, Carly saw that the entire gathering of right whales had surrounded Mother Earth, keeping a safe distance away, except for one—Otis—who was right there.

As soon as Otis spotted Carly on the bow, it was if the sadness lifted from his eyes. And at that same moment John said, "Stop that, Carly! You're projecting again."

Carly looked at John. "I don't think I am. And if possible, I think we should look into this."

"Look into what?" John questioned.

Carly continued, "I can understand him clearly, John. I really can. The Mother Earth and I are now Otis' mother. Just wait and see!

"John, I don't know if it is from all this—his birth, his mother dying, or his just being so young. It is not as if we are having an actual conversation, but more like we are connecting on a much deeper level of understanding. And as I get these feelings and visions from him, there seems to be a reaction of sorts. He understands what I am thinking, and I understand what he is thinking.

Now, stop talking. And remember, John, whales are smarter than we are."

CHAPTER 4

CONNECTIONS & UNDERSTANDING

Carly spent the entire day trying to decipher the thoughts in her head—some thoughts were her own while others seemed to belong to Otis. It was overwhelming. She stared at Otis as he floated beside Mother Earth, and then she looked out over the expanse to observe the vigil of the other whales.

Every now and again, a whale would swim alongside Otis, but Otis would just brush it aside. As time went by, Carly knew that Otis surely must be hungry, so she closed her eyes and concentrated as mightily as she could on that single thought.

And just as Carly opened her eyes again, she saw that another whale was beside Otis. And this time, Otis swam away with the adult whale. Carly was convinced that somehow the whales had heard her plea to take Otis for food, and she was also certain that Otis would return to her.

Carly was a scientist, a well-trained scientist, and she had been around the sea her entire life. She had heard stories of people feeling connected to the creatures of the sea, but she was not aware of any case where humans actually understood the animals. She knew it would not make any sense to anyone else; nevertheless, here she was, feeling as if she was sifting through a cloud, gathering small pieces of a puzzle trying to put together the whole picture.

While she was waiting for Otis to return, more and more images had filled Carly's head. As she concentrated on her thoughts, the full picture began coming into focus; and before long, she began seeing things more clearly.

Carly felt like she was making a connection with the other whales, too, and this caused her additional confusion. It was difficult trying to decipher the countless images, and her head began to hurt.

Otis and the other whale eventually returned to Mother Earth, and the other whale rose to the surface and gave Carly what appeared to be a knowing smile.

That night she needed some restful sleep— shielded away from everyone and everything including Otis—so she went to her cabin.

While she slept, the most vivid images invaded Carly's dreams. They were images of Mama being taken from the beach by a crane and work crew.

It was a terrifying sight, and Carly tossed and turned restlessly. It was as if she were seeing everything through the eyes of the other whales as they watched and mourned the loss of one of their own.

The images were so dramatic that Carly awoke in a fright. She sprang from her bed and ran half-dressed to the deck, arriving just in time to see Mama being removed from the beach.

As all of the whales floated at the water's surface watching what was happening on the beach, Carly wept. She wept not only for the loss of Mama, but also because she could feel the deep sorrow of all the whales. There absolutely *was* a connection.

As the sun rose, the sky was filled with all the beautiful colors that only God can make. John walked to the bow where Carly had fallen asleep while keeping vigil with the whales. John whispered, "What's going on?"

"I can understand them, John," she replied.

And as Carly spoke, a whale came alongside Mother Earth, waved a fin, and then dove deep into the water. Then another appeared, and then another. John quietly watched as whale after whale came alongside Mother Earth to say goodbye.

Bewildered, John said, "Well, that was weird."

And then one more whale came by, but this one stayed longer. Carly saw a clear image that this was the one that had taken Otis to eat yesterday.

The image from this whale was more like a video rather than just a snapshot. It was a series of images showing that Otis had learned what he needed to know in order to feed himself and that he would be just fine from here on. Carly smiled at her new ability and was comforted to know that Otis could find food for himself.

John was dumbfounded. Had he really just witnessed wild whales saying goodbye? As a matter a fact, the entire crew was rather dumbfounded. All the while, Carly smiled knowingly at Otis because they both understood.

By noontime, the sun had risen high in the sky, and it was time to consider the next move for Mother Earth and what to do with Otis. Since the other whales had moved off and Otis stayed nearby, what *were* they going to do with him, indeed?

John called a meeting in the conference room, and Captain Adare came down from the bridge to join them.

Captain Adare was a stocky man with short grey hair and a beard. Tanned and wrinkled from his many years at sea, he had a commanding presence, even though he stood only 5 feet 6 inches tall. Everyone on the ship unquestioningly followed the captain's orders. He just had that way about him.

Although Captain Adare appeared to be a salty, old sea dog, he was far from it. His rough exterior played right into the roll, but those closest to him knew that he was a softy. They also knew that he knew what he was talking about without question.

He was a wise man with good judgment, and his loyal crew followed every order. Captain Adare did not let everyone see this side of him, however. Most of his crew members had been with him for many years, and some for decades, so they knew him well.

But for Carly, John, and the other biologists, this was their first sailing with the captain. And since this was the first time that the captain had attended one of their meetings, they were quite nervous and uncertain of what he might say.

John was the first to speak. "Hello Captain."

The captain waved his hand stopping John in mid-sentence. And without a word, he simply crossed the room (as the crew cleared a path) and walked directly to Carly.

Standing at about the same height, Carly looked into the captain's steely eyes. She was afraid that he was going to call an end to the expedition.

Captain Adare returned Carly's gaze, and then he softened. He placed his hand on Carly's arm, smiled broadly, and hugged her.

Carly did not know how to react to this unexpected bear hug. All she could manage to do was laugh and cry at the same time.

Captain Adare embraced Carly and exclaimed, "In all my years at sea, I have wanted this! I have wished for this and knew it could happen. But I never dreamed that in my lifetime I would witness the joining of the land and the sea. We must see where all of this goes. Mother Earth is ready to go wherever she needs to go!"

Everyone began cheering and talking all at once, and someone unrolled a map across the table.

The captain let go of Carly and said, "Look girl! The heck with the rest! This is too important. We will scrap the Intracoastal trip, and, instead, we will follow the whales. We must see how this all plays out. My dear child, there is a connection and an understanding of something that is greater than we are!"

CHAPTER 5

FOLLOW THE LEADER

Everyone watched as John studied the map and then traced the whales' migration pattern southward along the coast to the warm waters of the Caribbean.

With so few right whales remaining, it has been well-known for many years that these creatures need to be protected. But really, once outside of the Intracoastal region, how does someone look after an 80-ton whale that has a mind of its own?

John drew two lines on the map. The first line represented the traditional migration pattern. The second line showed how the whales were currently staying close to the coast. It looked like they were trying to make it easy for the Mother Earth to follow them.

The captain also weighed in with his own experience of the migration patterns that he had witnessed, and then Carly joined in the conversation.

Carly pointed to the line that passed Cuba and

turned west toward the Gulf of Mexico. She said that she did not know how she knew it, but she just knew that the whales were changing their pattern so that the Mother Earth could stay with them, and the crew did not doubt her word because they all had watched as each whale—one by one—came to say goodbye to Carly and Mother Earth.

They all had observed Carly interact with Otis, and they all understood that there was something special between them. So, if Carly's instincts pointed them in that direction, well then, that was where they were going!

"Excellent!" Captain Adare exclaimed. "We will head that way in the morning. Start making preparations. I want designated shifts for lookouts. I want someone tracking with sonar. And I want you, Carly, on the bow or at the helm with me. The choice is yours, dear.

And, John, I want you to figure out what is going on here. I want to know more about this connection and what it all means."

At sunrise Mother Earth's crew was ready for action. The crew members were well rested; and after a hearty breakfast, they were prepared to begin what was to become a grand adventure.

The sonar technicians were already tracking the movements of the whales that had set out the day before—watching not only their heading, but also observing that the whales were traveling as a group.

While this is a fairly common occurrence in small groups, it had never been documented on such a large scale that seemed to include all of the North Atlantic right whales. But then again, nothing about how they have been acting lately was normal.

Mother Earth tracked the whales southward along the Florida coastline towards Saint Augustine. The whales were just now passing Amelia Island, home of the legendary town of Fernandina that, once upon a time, had been a secret pirate hideaway.

Today, instead of pirates, Fernandina is home to folks from all walks of life. It is a sea town whose residents delight in its pirate history just as much as in its modern fine dining. This will be the first stop for Mother Earth so that the crew can take on supplies, fuel, and additional equipment.

Carly climbed onto the deck at sun up just in time to see Otis surface beside Mother Earth. He swam directly to the bow and waited as Carly approached.

Carly had slept like a baby. Very few visions had interrupted her sleep as had happened the previous two nights. Last night had been absolutely peaceful, which Carly had needed more than she had realized.

When Carly first saw Otis, all seemed to be right with the world. But soon, the calm from the night before had disappeared, and her mind became jumbled with images and feelings.

The emotions were something new that had not been there before. But, just as the images had been unclear at first, these emotions were all muddled as well. And being flooded with so many emotions at once, Carly had difficulty sorting through them.

Ultimately, two stood out more clearly than the rest—affection and gratitude. As she gazed into his eyes, Carly understood that Otis was projecting his feelings of affection and gratitude to her.

As the crew powered up the ship's engines and hoisted the anchor from the muddy sea floor, Carly could hardly contain her excitement.

John arrived on deck just as the propellers started turning and Mother Earth got under way. He immediately headed toward Carly, and with a cheerful, "Good morning, Otis!" he raised his coffee cup to greet the whale. Otis seemed to acknowledge John, but John brushed it off as unimportant…at least for now. Then John finally asked Carly what had been on his mind for a while, "Carly, are you sure you feel some form of connection with Otis and the others?"

"Oh! Yes!" was Carly's emphatic reply.

John continued, "Well, we are picking up some equipment and a new crew member in Fernandina."

Carly looked questioningly at John as he spoke.

"Carly, if there is some form of connection between you and Otis, we certainly need to figure it out."

Carly nodded her head in agreement while keeping her eyes fixed on Otis as he swam along the surface nearby.

John continued, "We will be picking up a neuropsychologist who specializes in marine-life brain patterns. Her name is Eleanor Thrush, and she has been studying marine mammals for over two decades. I want her to work closely with you and Otis.

Eleanor's job will be to see whether there are any changes in your and Otis' brain functions when you are near each other."

John explained to Carly that he had been unable to sleep all night after witnessing the whales' goodbyes, so he had contacted some people at Florida State University Marine Biology program and asked for their top person specializing in the brain activity of marine mammals.

He was then directed to Eleanor Thrush who was

considered to be the top in her field; and after a brief email exchange with her, she had agreed to meet John and the others in Fernandina.

Expressing her doubts to John, she made it clear that while the behavior of these whales was odd indeed, she was highly skeptical that there could be any actual "connection" between Carly and Otis; that is, other than everyone's desire for it to be true. Eleanor was confident that she would be proving that this was all nonsense.

Mother Earth was underway, and Otis swam right alongside. Carly sat on the bow to watch Otis play and to brush up on her knowledge of right whales.

According to the book she was reading, it is believed that the name "right whale" came from the ancient whale hunters claiming these were the right whales to kill on a hunt because they swam so slowly and spent much of their time at the surface or doing shallow dives before going deep for up to 20 minutes at a time. This made them perfect targets for whalers. And sadly, that was why Otis had been Number 36, but was now Number 35.

Carly smiled as she realized that Otis's birth was an amazing blessing. It showed that the whales were still breeding and attempting to come back from total extinction. It became clear that life always tries to survive.

Carly wrote in her journal as she watched Otis. He seemed to be the normal size—around 13 feet long and weighing about one ton. Otis was a little on the small side, but still a giant animal that will get only bigger. Adult right whales can grow to 60 feet long, weigh up to 80 tons, and live to be more than 70 years old. Their gigantic adult size was evident from

Otis' mother. And as Carly's thoughts drifted back to Mama, more images flashed through her mind.

As if looking through Mama's eyes, Carly saw the beach, she saw the sharks, and she also saw a sky that turned almost green with air so thick that Carly started to feel as if she were choking.

The vision not only brought a feeling of intense sadness, but also physical sensations. Suddenly, she found it difficult to breathe and to see, and she began feeling queasy. The overwhelming nature of this felt like an out-of-body experience. Carly had become Mama for an instant, and then the sensations disappeared just as quickly as they had begun.

Carly sat on the ship's bow staring intently at Otis as he skimmed for food taking in zooplankton by the ton to fill his growing body. Occasionally, Otis would dive deeply and feed like a wild boy—chasing down every microscopic morsel of food that he could find.

Her journal was always nearby, and now Carly began to fill it with the images that she saw. As a scientist herself, Carly knew the importance of keeping good documentation. And since they would be meeting Eleanor Thrush soon, Carly had a pretty good idea of just what questions Eleanor would ask. Or at least Carly thought she knew.

Time passes very slowly when traveling at six miles per hour on the water. The head sonar technician Tim came up on deck and approached Carly and John. Tim was a lanky, bearded young man who was just happy to be out of the Navy and to be able to wear cut-off jeans and flip flops all day, and he brought them some interesting news.

Tim explained that it was widely known that right whales do not travel in large groups. But this time they were traveling in an unusually large group, which is why their gathering at the beach was such a surprise. Tim told Carly and John that the whales have continued to stay together and that they were not far away—only a few miles ahead and moving slowly enough for Mother Earth to easily shadow them. It also appeared that Otis was tracking perfectly parallel to Mother Earth even when he swam deep.

Tim had also identified one whale that appeared to be the leader of the pack as well—a colossal right whale that easily surpassed the presumed maximum size of 80 tons. Its signature on the sonar screen seemed to also suggest that it was at least ten feet longer than the next largest whale in the group and possibly an additional 10 tons heavier, too.

John exclaimed, "I think we have found the leader. Now it's time to play! Come on, Carly!"

Carly laughed, and she thanked Tim for the news as he disappeared back inside the ship.

Then she asked John, "Time to play?"

"Yes. It's time to play Follow the Leader. Don't you remember playing that game as a child?" John replied.

"No. I didn't really play with other kids very much. I was always on the water," Carly responded a bit sharply.

John just laughed and walked away mumbling to himself, "No wonder she talks to whales."

As Carly was half pouting at John's last remark, she caught Otis's eye. Otis looked like he had a smirk on his whale-sized little face. Carly just groaned, "Oh, no! Not you, too!" And then she grinned and sat down to do some more writing about her visions.

On the bridge, John greeted Captain Adare and

informed him about the new crew member, Eleanor Thrush. When the captain asked what kind of person she was, John simply shrugged his shoulders and said, "I have no clue. But, apparently, she thinks this is all a bunch of nonsense. But, hey! If she truly is as good as her reputation states, then maybe we can find out for sure what is going on."

Then John explained what he had learned from Tim. He described to the captain how the whales were staying grouped together and seemed to have a leader. He also said that they appeared to be traveling in a way to keep Mother Earth nearby.

The captain just kept shaking his head saying, "This is something special, John. But first we are going to have to take a break from this little game of Follow the Leader. We are about to sail into the Fernandina Harbor. Go down to the deck and get ready to set some lines."

Carly saw the harbor up ahead, and she began feeling like Otis was sharing a vision with her. As they approached the harbor, Otis kept a comfortable distance at the starboard side of the ship. And soon Mother Earth was pulling up to the dock and being tied off. Just as the ladder was set, a woman came walking toward the gangway.

A tall, Irish woman with reddish-blonde hair came to the ladder shouting, "John! John!"

John peered over the ladder, "Well, you must be Ellie?"

"No. It's Eleanor," she curtly replied,

Carly warily shouted, "Hello, Ellie!"

As Eleanor stared up at Carly and John, Otis exhaled through his blowhole and greeted Eleanor with a big splash that soaked her from head to toe.

Eleanor was not pleased at all, but then she saw Otis. He had surfaced in the slip beside Mother Earth, which left Eleanor stunned and speechless.

CHAPTER 6

PROPER INTRODUCTIONS

Eleanor, along with all of her luggage, computers, and research equipment boarded the Mother Earth. She filled not just one cabin, but also space in a second cabin as well.

After stowing her gear in her quarters and freshening up a bit, Eleanor reemerged. John smiled as he and Carly walked over to greet her.

John welcomed his fellow scientist with a firm, friendly handshake and thanked her for agreeing to join them on this the trip.

Eleanor, however, appeared to be stern and a little stand-offish. She preferred to work with animals because she disliked people, but no one could ever understand why.

She was attractive, athletic, and professional, but she seemed to be a little too perfect as if there was no room for error in her world. Everything had to be perfect; and if it wasn't perfect, then she couldn't be bothered with it. Her entire demeanor seemed as if a person's image and status were paramount, and she made no bones about it. She also believed that this whole concept of communicating with whales was absurd, and she was going to prove it.

To John, Carly, and the captain, Eleanor did not seem to be a very pleasant person. She acted as though she wanted to be someone else. She tried too hard to fit the role of a perfectionist. Every detail had to be flawless. It was kind of unnerving to be around; but come what may, they needed her, and so they looked past her haughtiness hoping that eventually the reasons for her behavior would come to light.

Eleanor, or Ellie as the crew referred to her, did not care for the size of Mother Earth—it was too small for her liking. She was accustomed to much larger vessels with much more modern equipment and wondered to herself, "What in the world did I do to deserve this? I worked like this when I was Carly's age. I am better than this now."

But, in the back of her mind she also remembered that it was kind of fun, too. But she would never admit that out loud. Oh no!

As the crew was coming and going with preparations for this expedition, the captain called the team of scientists together for a meeting to announce his plans to continue tracking the whales, introduce Eleanor to everyone, and clarify each person's job for this voyage.

As Carly started walking inside for the meeting, she looked across the water and saw the hump of another right whale not far from the dock. Carly sensed a feeling of extreme hunger and knew it was coming from Otis, so she just looked at him and thought, "Go, baby." And surely enough, Otis dipped down and went to meet the other whale.

Just then Tim yelled, "Hey Carly! There is another whale over there!" Carly replied with a smile, "Gee! Thanks for the heads up."

The meeting was similar to the one the day before. They reviewed the plan to follow the whales, mostly for Eleanor's benefit, but some new information was also provided.

The rest of the crew learned for the first time that the whales were definitely traveling as a group, that they appeared to have a leader, and that they were keeping Mother Earth within close proximity.

Even Eleanor who had been studying these amazing creatures ever since she was Carly's age was astonished to learn of this uncharacteristic behavior. However, she could never let on that she was fascinated. After all, she was here to prove that this was all just nonsense.

John introduced Eleanor to the crew, and each crew member greeted Eleanor with a smile and a friendly handshake—everyone, that is, but Tim.

Tim had to do it. He had to be the goof. He gave Eleanor a great big hug. He wrapped his lanky arms around her and exclaimed, "Welcome aboard, Ellie!"

As his sweaty, shirtless body covered Eleanor's clean, crisp suit, she squirmed like a fish out of water. It was an amusing sight.

Her arms were pinned down by her sides, and she clearly was not amused. (But deep down inside she giggled...just a little bit.) At one time, Eleanor did know how to have fun, but now was not the time. She had appearances to keep up.

Eleanor quickly regained her composure and

pushed Tim away stating clearly and forcefully, "It's Eleanor, not Ellie! And I would appreciate everyone remembering that!"

There was a collective "Ohhh!" and everyone straightened up, even Captain Adare.

Eleanor went on to explain why she was here. "While you all seem to believe that there is some form of cosmic communication or super-natural understanding going on here, I assure you that it cannot be true.

"I have been doing this for 23 years, and I am quite certain that this is nothing more than all of you wishing it to be true. But I am a scientist, and if there is something here, we will get to the bottom of it in short order. While I agree that the whales' recent behavior is strange, I'm sure that it can be explained"...or so she thought.

"We are going to start with a behavioral analysis, which means that we are going to evaluate what we already know against what is currently happening. I have heard of these visions, so we will place a few sensors on the whale. What do you call him?"

The crew shouted in unison, "Otis."

Eleanor continued, "We need clear readings on Otis and clear readings on you, too, Carly."

Carly looked a little surprised to hear that she was going to be a lab rat as well. But sure! If her baby Otis was to be, then so would she. It was time to discover if there was something more to this and why this was happening at all. Carly smiled and waved her hand in agreement.

As the meeting drew to a close, Captain Adare made one last announcement, "I do not know when we will be ashore again, so tonight you are free to do as you please. Make sure you get all of your partying out of your system tonight. We hit the seas at sun up, so just keep that in mind.

"Dismissed."

After the meeting, John approached Eleanor and said, "We should get to know each other."

Eleanor looked at him and curtly replied, "Excuse me! You are not my type. I date only people with money."

John started laughing, "Umm…You are not my type either. And that is not what I meant, but I'll keep that in mind. I simply meant that we all should get to know each other since we will be working closely together."

Embarrassed, Eleanor could muster only, "Yes. Sure. Sorry."

And John thought to himself, "Boy! This is going to be a lot of fun."

John and Eleanor caught up with the captain and Carly, and John suggested, "Let's hit the Palace! Did you know that it is the oldest bar in Florida! We can all relax and get to know one another."

Tim overheard this and chimed in, "Sounds great! Let's go!" So, they all headed down to the pier.

Carly noticed that Otis had not returned and that she wasn't getting any visions from him either. Although she was somewhat concerned, she decided that she needed the break…and a drink.

As they left the marina, John explained that the Palace was the oldest continually operating bar in the state and that the mayor of Fernandina was also the bartender there—all adding to the lore of the town.

As they walked by the pirate statue at the front door, it was clear that the Palace itself was nothing really special, just a very old bar, but it had a certain air about it. And Eleanor was the first to complain about the air, "Eww! People smoke in here!"

Both the captain and John laughed, "Well, *yeah*! It *is* a bar."

After getting a table and a pitcher of beer, the personal stories began. To break the ice, the captain started the conversation. He talked about his life—his decades at sea, the many shores he had visited, and the problems he had avoided because his mistress was the sea. He even talked a little about the magic he had witnessed these past few days.

With the second pitcher of beer, Tim shared his story. He was from a little town in Idaho and had joined the Navy to get away because he had felt that he just didn't fit in—he was not a farmer, he was a goof; he was an adventurer in search of an adventure.

He soon discovered that he disliked being in the Navy—the rules, the uniforms, and hair cut. Oh! That haircut was the reason he completed his four years and did not re-enlist. Now he just wants to be Captain Adare, and he slapped the captain on the back as he said it. The captain chuckled, "In your dreams."

Along with the third pitcher of beer, Carly told her story. She reflected on her childhood and her lifelong connection with the sea and its inhabitants.

She described how she recently began seeing images in her mind that she sensed were being projected from Otis' mother. It was as though she was seeing the world through the mother whale's eyes. Carly also described feeling the whale's pain during the shark attack. Then after Mama's death, she began sensing images from the baby whale.

And most recently, she was not only seeing

images, but also sensing feelings and emotions from other whales, too. As Carly recounted her story, everyone hung onto her every word—everyone but one person, Eleanor. Eleanor was not impressed.

As the fourth pitcher was being served, John motioned to Eleanor to tell her story. Eleanor began by making it clear that she was here only at the request of the university and that she had put aside more important research in order to be here. She said that she was planning to quickly complete this project and return to the more important things that she left behind and that she considered this trip to be a mere distraction and a totally unnecessary endeavor. She assumed that she would easily disprove all of this and then be on her way.

However, as she spoke, she realized that deep down inside she missed this. She missed her time at sea, missed the fun and the excitement, and missed the feeling of being alive that comes only from truly living and not from some exercise class. Deep down inside, she realized that she wanted and needed this trip because she had somehow lost herself through the years. But then she thought that was nothing more than a stupid notion and dismissed it before saying any more.

The captain excused himself and headed to the bar just as another pitcher of beer arrived at the table.

Finally, it was John's turn. He told everyone about the death of his two-year-old daughter and how his wife, his childhood sweetheart whom he had married after graduating college, couldn't handle the loss of their only child. The divorce had crushed him, and now he was set on being on the water and keeping a distance from people so that he would not get hurt again. For John, being at sea was akin to having a giant moat around his heart.

The more they drank, the more personal their stories became, and both ladies were visibly shocked at hearing of the loss of John's little girl.

Just then the captain returned with three rounds of tequila shots, "I order you all to suck them down and smile about it!"

So after a hearty "Bottoms up!" the tequila went down, and then they headed back to the ship. The walk back seemed to take much longer somehow.

When they reached the ship, a visibly tipsy Carly started looking around for Otis. She even got down on her hands and knees, looked at the water, and started calling, "O-tis! O-tis!"

Equally tipsy Eleanor scoffed, "That whale cannot hear you, let alone understand you."

Suddenly, Otis surfaced and exhaled water all over Eleanor for the second time that day! A shocked Eleanor stood there, stomped her feet like a child, and screamed, "I hate this!"

Apparently, not everybody hated it because everyone else erupted into roars of laughter, and Otis started bobbing his head up and down. Now it seems that proper introductions had finally been made all the way around.

The evening was over and it was time for bed. Carly reached down and rubbed Otis's head. This was the first time she had touched him; and as she did, she got a very strong image from him. This image was similar to the one she received earlier—she felt a terrible emptiness and smelled an awful stench, almost like the smell of death.

CHAPTER 7

OH! COOL! NEW HEAD GEAR!

The next morning it was clear that the crew was feeling the effects of the previous night's festivities. Even Eleanor who generally wore business suits was dressed like she had just rolled out of bed—wearing a t-shirt, shorts, and flip-flops.

The sun had risen hours ago, and the only person who seemed unaffected was Captain Adare, but somehow that seemed to be normal for a lifelong seaman.

Tim walked into the sonar room as the crew cast the lines off of Mother Earth and they continued their southbound journey. Otis took his position alongside Mother Earth, swimming methodically and in line with the ship.

Eleanor approached Carly and asked her to explain what her visions were like, and Carly gladly told her all about them.

Carly explained that how in the beginning the

images were all muddled as if in a fog, and then how the images gradually became clearer. She described how sharply she could feel the pain and fear that Mama had felt as the sharks were attacking her and how she felt like she was seeing the world through Mama's eyes.

Carly recounted the arrival of all of the other right whales and the manner in which they all had seemed to pay their respects as Mama died on the beach that night.

Then she described the odd pangs of hunger she had felt and realized that this strange new sensation had come from Otis.

She told Eleanor how she had imagined herself calling to the other whales for help and how one whale must have "heard" her plea and had come and taken Otis to teach him how to find food.

This all seemed a pretty bizarre to Eleanor, but she listened carefully and took lots of notes. Carly continued talking not only about the visions, but also about the senses that crept in with each image. It was clear that it was becoming easier for Carly and Otis to understand each other. And now the visions flashed quickly, and each image was accompanied by feelings and needs.

Eleanor wanted to believe this child. She called Carly a child because to Eleanor's skeptical nature, Carly was just that. But the soft side of Eleanor, the side that yearned to be her old self, wanted to believe Carly. So, Eleanor decided that this situation needed much more studying.

She asked Carly to wear a portable EEG (electroencephalogram) monitor so that Carly's brain waves could be monitored throughout the entire ship.

From the beginning, Carly had suspected that this was a possibility, and she eagerly agreed.

Then Eleanor asked how to fit a monitor on Otis. Now *that* was a good question. They both sat there for a bit pondering exactly how to make that happen, and then they burst into laughter at the idea of a headset like Carly's sitting on Otis' head.

A right whale's head is about one-third of its total body length, and its brain is huge. It is unknown how much of their brain they actually use, but it is believed that as much as 50 percent of their brain is in use at any given time.

Unfortunately, the monitor that Eleanor brought was designed for a whale that is kept in captivity, so this unit could never work on a whale in the open ocean. So they called John to discuss their predicament and to see if he had any ideas for creating a monitoring device that would fit Otis.

John left Tim in the sonar room and headed to the mess hall, which was now being used as Eleanor's laboratory. When he arrived, John gave an update on the whales' current position—they were just five miles ahead of Mother Earth and still moving steadily to keep their distance constant. However, there was one new development: The leader had dropped back and was now swimming about a mile out and parallel to Mother Earth. Why was it keeping its distance? Well, only Carly knows!

When John spied Carly's new head gear, he laughed, "You look just like a telephone operator on steroids!" And to a degree, he was right. Carly's headset had flashing lights, bands, and sensors all over her head, but it was on and working. The first step was to get a base reading, so Eleanor instructed

Carly to make notes of the date and time of all whale-related activity. This would be easy for Carly because she had been recording their every move already.

John looked at the apparatus that Eleanor had brought for Otis and started laughing. He knew there was no way this contraption was going to work because there were too many straps, wires, and gadgets attached to it. He suggested that instead of using one large device, they build several smaller ones with individual EEG units. He also suggested that each device be self powered and self contained inside of a box about the size of a large shoe box. He also thought that each box should have a recessed barb mechanism and include a pad on the bottom on which to apply a strong adhesive.

John's design concept became clear as he showed them a recent photo of Otis. All right whales have trademark markings on the tops of their heads, and John's photo showed that Otis was starting to get his. These bumps, called callosities, are sections of rough skin similar to giant calluses and are believed to have no nerve endings; however, their specific purpose was still unknown. Otis had six of these forming at this time, and John felt that this would be the ideal place to attach the modular EEG units.

Carly, Eleanor, and John were all in agreement. And with the help of a few crew members, they disassembled the headsets that Eleanor had brought, re-configured everything as John had suggested, and soon they had had six self-powered EEG units in waterproof boxes that could be attached by both small barbs and extremely tough glue. Now the question was how to get to Otis and attach the boxes.

"Easy! We cut the engines, and then I get down

on the dive platform and call Otis to me. When he comes alongside the platform, I attach the devices!" Carly suggested.

John and Eleanor looked at each other in astonishment. And despite all that John had witnessed on this trip, Carly's idea still sounded crazy.

Nevertheless, they decided to try Carly's idea, and Carly and John headed topside. Meanwhile, Eleanor stayed in the lab to watch for any abnormal readings on her instruments when Carly "called" Otis.

First, John stopped to see Captain Adare and explain their plans, and then the captain cut the engines to allow Mother Earth to drift.

Next, Carly stood on the deck of the ship, closed her eyes, and started concentrating on Otis. She envisioned him swimming to the dive platform, and then she pictured the boxes being placed on his head. She was careful to make these her only thoughts. And before long, John tapped Carly on the shoulder and pointed toward the water. Carly opened her eyes and, sure enough, Otis was right there next to the dive platform.

Carly climbed down to the platform to greet Otis. She knelt down and gently rubbed his head near his eyes. She identified the callosities and touched them as she envisioned herself placing the boxes on them. Otis did not move. And then an image flashed through Carly's mind as if she was seeing through Otis's eyes. It was an image of the boxes being placed on his head. Otis had understood! Carly called to John to bring the boxes down to her.

Even though these were patches of rough skin, Otis was still a baby after all. Since he was still not fully developed, Carly thought that attaching the boxes may hurt him a little. So, Carly envisioned a physical pain, and then the pain being soothed. She concentrated on that thought, and shortly the same thought came back to her. Otis had understood! So she began the process of carefully attaching the first of the six boxes.

At first, Otis flinched a good bit, but then he calmed down quickly and allowed Carly to continue. Carly carefully attached the second, third, fourth, and fifth boxes. However, to attach the sixth box, Carly had to stretch out all the way across the top of Otis. It was a little daunting, and the waves were somewhat rougher than usual.

Meanwhile, John had been videotaping the entire process. And just as Carly stretched across Otis to reach the sixth callosity, a loud thud suddenly jolted Mother Earth, and Carly toppled into the ocean alongside of Otis.

Being an experienced ocean swimmer, Carly quickly surfaced. She saw that Mother Earth was taking another blow to her starboard side, which pushed her farther away. Otis quickly dove beneath the surface and left Carly treading water. Fortunately, Carly was still holding the sixth box in her hands.

Carly suddenly realized what was happening. This other whale thought that she was hurting Otis.

The massive right whale was heading straight towards Carly. Right whales have no teeth; but if their fins would hit a human, it would crush the person in seconds. Carly had a look of sheer terror, and the whale looked angry. However, before the massive whale could get any closer to Carly, Otis surfaced and positioned himself between Carly and the aggressor in order to take any blow from the other whale.

Carly swam feverishly towards Mother Earth while Otis protected her. As she neared the dive platform, she looked back at the surfacing behemoth.

As Carly looked into the whales eyes, she instantly sensed a reaction of "you do not understand." In reply, Carly conveyed a feeling of understanding. She visualized images of the exchange with Otis, and she conveyed her fear and respect. With that, the colossal whale hesitated and calmed down. And then both the other whale and Otis swam slowly towards Carly.

John was screaming from the deck, and the crew was scrambling for life preservers and getting ready to jump in after her when Carly yelled, "No!"

Before long the two whales had reached Carly. She could have been easily crushed, but Carly reached out to touch the giant of the sea just below its eye.

As she touched the whale, Carly again saw the sky of green and a world devoid of life, and she also smelled the stench of death.

This time the sensations were so overwhelming that Carly's mind started to spin; and just as she began to lose consciousness, Otis swam beneath her and very gently lifted her body onto his back and carried her safely to Mother Earth's dive platform where John was waiting to pull her aboard.

Then both Otis and the other whale disappeared into the depths.

CHAPTER 8

THIS CANNOT BE RIGHT

John placed the unconscious Carly on the dive platform and performed some basic CPR. Eventually, Carly began to cough up water, and John breathed a sigh of relief.

Although Carly was still a bit incoherent, she clung tightly to the sixth box. As soon as she was able, John helped Carly to her feet.

Eleanor ran toward them yelling, "What the heck was that!"

John stared at Eleanor as he and Carly climbed the ladder to the deck. When they reached the top, he sat Carly in a chair as another crew member brought her something to drink. John looked at Eleanor, "What are you talking about? She almost died."

"We *all* almost died!" replied Eleanor.

Crew members were running all about the deck. A few were lowered over the side of the ship to assess the damage from the whale's attack. Captain Adare came down from the bridge, and Tim emerged from the main cabin. They all converged around Carly who was still extremely shaken.

Captain Adare began, "Now we have an adventure! That was the first ever recorded right whale attack, and we are here to tell the tale.

"Now Tim, why didn't you warn us about that whale coming in so close?"

Feeling a little embarrassed at the moment, Tim meekly replied, "Captain, I am sorry. I was paying such close attention to Carly and Otis, and the big one came from so far below. I didn't even see it. Do you think Mother Earth is still seaworthy?"

"Sure she is boy! It will take more than a few bumps to damage her!" the captain boasted.

"A few bumps?" Eleanor exclaimed. "We were just hit by an 80-ton whale! But really, that is not important. What *is* important is what we registered from both Carly's head gear and the five boxes on Otis. The readings are off the charts! Carly, I need to know what you experienced. Come with me."

"Hold on there!" John interrupted. "Carly is not going anywhere except to bed. And Tim, you had better get back to your sonar and keep an eye on those two. And as for you, Captain, well, you just go do your captain stuff."

Then John picked up Carly in his arms, carried her down to her cabin, and placed her on her bed.

Carly looked up at a John with deeply saddened eyes and with a shaky voice said, "John, I think I know why this is all happening, and I am scared." And with that, she fell into a deep sleep.

John headed to Eleanor's laboratory. As he walked in, he noticed the reams of paper spread all over the tables and asked, "Is this all from earlier?"

"It went nuts, John! This cannot be right," replied Eleanor.

"There is too much of a coincidence. The readings show that there was only a fraction of a second between the time when Carly's brain pattern increased and when Otis' increased, and vice versa. This just cannot be right!" said a puzzled Eleanor.

"Why not?" John questioned, "Because it would mean there was some kind of connection?"

Eleanor stared at John and replied, "Yes, John. That is what it shows...at least on the surface. But this just cannot be right."

John pointed to the mass of scrambled lines on a large section of paper, "What is that?"

"That is from Carly, and it shows that her brain went briefly into some sort of a hyper-drive."

John wondered aloud, "Hmmm. Maybe that is why she said she knows why this is all happening and that she is scared"

Eleanor looked at him sternly and asked, "Where is she? I need answers right now! We need to get to the bottom of this!"

John firmly countered, "Relax. She is resting and this can wait."

Again, Eleanor stood there firmly and defiantly. She was not accustomed to being told to relax, and she had no tolerance for people who did not follow her orders.

Truthfully, Eleanor did not know how to handle being told to relax. She had forgotten how to relax. She had forgotten how to be herself. And deep down inside, she knew that she had also lost her empathy somewhere along the way.

John looked at her and smiled. He could see that

she was experiencing some kind of inner turmoil. He had heard through the grapevine that Eleanor had once been the Ellie that they all called her. She had been a vivacious young lady much like Carly.

As he walked past Eleanor, John grinned and shook his head. He half expected to see Otis come out of nowhere and blow water on her again.

John met Captain Adare in the sitting room. The captain assured him that the ship was fine—just a little banged up—and that he believed that the whale's "bump" was more of a warning rather than an all-out attack because if that whale had wanted to sink Mother Earth, she easily could have done so.

John informed the captain that something was actually happening between Carly and Otis and that even Eleanor was starting to see it, but Eleanor still had questions that needed answers.

Tim came out of the sonar room with an update on the whales, "Oh! There you both are. It looks like Otis is coming back to the ship, and that big, old whale is keeping its distance now."

"Great!" said the captain. "Let's head toward Otis and get this girl-and-whale show back into motion.

John, how long do you think Carly will be out?"

"I have no idea, Captain, but let's get moving!"

CHAPTER 9

SLEEPLESS SLEEP

Mother Earth quickly caught up to Otis and started towards the other whales as if nothing had happened. The Old Whale kept its one-mile distance off the starboard side as Otis and the ship continued southward along the coast.

Eleanor was closely monitoring the EEG readings from Carly and Otis. Soon she discovered that while Carly was sleeping, her brain was not showing normal sleeping patterns; instead, her patterns were more like someone in deep thought.

Time passed slowly that day. Everyone was still a bit shaken over the incident of the Old Whale ramming Mother Earth. It was as if it had been trying to stop the interaction between Carly and Otis. It was a deliberate act that had almost killed Carly. Had it not been for Otis, Carly surely would have drowned.

John kept a watchful eye as Otis swam beside the ship. He also scanned the horizon for signs of the Old Whale. He did not want to see that behemoth again anytime soon. Tim occasionally radioed John to update the whales' position as they maintained their southern route along the Florida coast. Before long they were passing Daytona Beach and heading into some of the most beautiful waters that the Atlantic Ocean has to offer.

The water in this area of the Atlantic is a beautiful blue reflection of the sky. The water here is quite different from the water in the north where it appears to be brown and dirty, even though it actually is no different. However, the sand and the beaches here are much different—soft and almost white, not course and tan as it is in the north. The Florida coastline is truly beautiful.

Captain Adare was in his element, steering Mother Earth along her merry journey. It all seemed pretty normal to him.

As the day passed and sunset approached, Mother Earth was nearing Cape Canaveral, the launching pad for all of America's greatest space missions. This is the ideal location for space launches because one can see for tens of miles in any direction. The weather is always warm, and the sky is typically cloudless and blue. And on this particular night, the crew would personally witness human greatness. Space X would be launching a new satellite system tonight.

Suddenly, Mother Earth's radio blared loudly. They were five miles from Cape Canaveral and were being instructed to halt and wait for the launch. So, stop and wait they did.

Seeing the light from a million-horsepower rocket in the distance in the pitch black of night is like seeing the sun rise out of the ground.

And although they were five miles away, the

entire crew could feel in their chests the thumping of the rocket's engines.

Ellie had come outside to behold some of the wonders that man had created. Even she was astonished at the realization that, of all of earth's inhabitants over millions of years, only the most recent generations have been the ones to have ever escaped the atmospheric confines of this spaceship called Planet Earth.

As the crew watched from the deck, Tim noticed something else—the whales had also stopped. It was as if they, too, were watching the escape of mankind into outer space.

As the rocket passed through the atmosphere and into space without a hitch, everyone aboard Mother Earth cheered another human achievement.

By now it was getting late, so Captain Adare ordered the crew to set anchor here for the night.

John was concerned about Carly, and he thought that perhaps Otis may be worried as well because Otis had been circling the ship all evening as if looking for some sign of her.

John walked to the stern and shouted, "I doubt you can understand me, but she is fine. I am going to check on her now. You get some rest, young man!"

Then John laughed and wondered as he walked into the cabin, "Did I just talk to a whale?"

As he stood in the doorway of Carly's room, he thought she had a childlike innocence about her. John had never had any more children, and it seemed that family life was just not in the cards for him. Perhaps that is why he had taken Carly under his wing.

As John was about to leave, a hand lightly touched his shoulder. It was Eleanor. She looked over his shoulder at Carly and whispered, "I need to check her vitals. The readings I have been getting are off the chart." But Eleanor didn't sound like she normally did; she actually sounded likable.

As Eleanor walked over to Carly, John could not help but wonder what made Eleanor this way. He could see the softer side of her at times, especially at moments like this, but then noticed that when others were around, she was all about "the image." John wondered how someone could be so at odds with themselves. "Oh well," he thought as he stood beside her and stared at Carly.

Ellie stroked Carly's hair and whispered, "Everything is ok, child."

Carly seemed to hear her, but had a pained look on her face as if she was trying to comprehend something, yet was struggling with it.

John stayed for a few more minutes before saying goodnight, and then he left the two women alone.

Early the next morning, Mother Earth was cruising down the coast again. After watching Otis swim alongside for a while, John went to check on Carly. He walked into the cabin and found Ellie slumped over the table fast asleep with her hand resting on Carly's arm. "Maybe this woman has a soul after all," he thought.

When he touched Eleanor's shoulder, she awoke, but Carly still did not move. Caught in what she perceived to be a moment of weakness, Eleanor hastily stood and left the room, and John sat down beside Carly.

Captain Adare was busy on the bridge, and Tim was in the sonar room tracking the whales while the rest of the crew was bustling about taking care of the other duties aboard the vessel. By nightfall they should be nearing Miami, but only time and tide would tell.

As the day drew on, Carly remained asleep, but had become very restless. She tossed and turned as if in a sleepless sleep. Occasionally, she would repeat, "No. No. No." But she said nothing else.

The rest of the day and night passed without incident. The Old Whale stayed a safe, steady mile away, and the rest of the whales maintained their southerly heading along the coast toward the city of Miami. And all the while, Otis, the lovable juvenile, stayed right alongside, never moving far from Mother Earth and Carly.

CHAPTER 10

THE AWAKENING

The sun rose over the horizon as Mother Earth approached Miami. It was going to be a warm day. Sunrise here was like no other place—with oranges and blues in every rich tone of the spectrum, it is obvious that only God could design them. And unless one sees it in person, one cannot fully imagine it.

After John dutifully checked on Otis, he decided to check on Eleanor, too. She had been locked away in her lab studying readout after readout.

As he entered the room, he could tell she was a bit frantic. Her instruments were going wild again as the pens were sketching lines at an amazing rate on the paper.

John stood quietly in the doorway watching Eleanor run frantically from machine to machine. Eventually, he asked her if something was wrong.

"I am not exactly sure if anything is actually wrong," she said.

John was surprised by her answer and wondered to himself, "Wow! There is something that she doesn't know?"

Just then Tim and a concerned-looking captain came down the hallway. The captain pointed to Eleanor's lab and said, "Good morning! We need to talk. Get in there."

Tim began, "That big whale is alongside us again, and Otis seems to be staying between it and us acting as a buffer."

The captain smiled, "I knew I liked that little boy! Is the other whale a threat?"

"No. It's been there for awhile," Tim replied.

"Tim, how long?" Eleanor asked as she pointed at the printouts.

"About 45 minutes," he replied.

Eleanor started writing on the printouts and punching numbers on her calculator. The men just watched her until she eventually turned and said, "Look at this!" as she handed them the printouts.

Shrugging their shoulders, they all asked at once, "Look at what?"

"At the time stamps! This is Carly's brain pattern. It started accelerating 45 minutes ago."

As they were reviewing the readings, Eleanor's EEG machine suddenly slowed and returned to a normal rhythm.

Tim radioed to the sonar room, but he was sure that he already knew the answer, "Where is the Old Whale now?"

"It moved away and is now heading back out," was the crackled reply.

They stared at each other in bewilderment. Had that just really happened?

Startled, they all jumped at once when a voice from behind them asked, "Hey! What are you all doing?" It was Carly.

They turned and saw a refreshed Carly standing in the doorway. She walked in and hugged each one warmly—the kind of hug you give when you haven't seen someone in a long time.

Then she stopped and looked at Eleanor and said, "You were wrong. I now know what this is all about. But first, I need to eat."

The others exclaimed together, "You have to tell us now!"

"You won't like it," Carly replied. "Can we please talk about it over some food. I'm so hungry. John, how long have I been in bed?"

"Two days," he replied.

As the coffee was brewing, Eleanor showed Carly the printouts and pointed, "Here is your brain activity, and here is Otis' activity. Do you see how they match?"

Carly responded very matter of factly, "Yes. I do. And now let me explain."

"The Old Whale will be coming close again soon. We need to attach the sixth box to her."

John immediately interrupted, "Not on your life! It almost killed you!"

"It's all right, John. She didn't understand before and was just protecting Otis. But I've talked to her. Well, sort of talked to her. I can communicate with them. I understand the visions, the feelings, and the physical sensations. And they can understand me in the same way."

The captain smiled as he listened to Carly while John and Tim shook their heads in disbelief.

Eleanor was the only one to respond, "Carly, have you gone mad? At one time in my life, I would have believed you. But after all I have experienced, there is no such thing as what you are describing. There is just no way that this is possible."

"Relax, Ellie!" The captain spoke up. "Why is it not possible? Because we haven't seen it before? Is it not possible because it has not happened to us? Is it not possible because we have never heard of it?

"Let me tell you kids something. I have seen things I cannot explain. I have been all around the globe and have seen far more of it than all of you combined, and yet I have seen maybe only one-tenth of the planet. And in that one-tenth, I have witnessed things I cannot explain—things like Carly and Otis, let alone all of the other whales gathered here.

"Did we not just sail past Cape Canaveral? Did you all not stand on the deck and watch that rocket soar through the confines of the earth's atmosphere into outer space? Don't you understand? Just 100 years before the first rocket was ever launched, people thought flight was just a fantasy. And many generations before that, people thought the world was flat.

"However, in the here and now, we all wish for the ability to communicate with other species."

As he gently hugged Carly and gave her a fatherly kiss on her forehead, the captain continued, "This young lady and that young whale out there are going to change the world.

"So Ellie, you need to lose that self-righteous attitude and understand that your job is to not disprove it, but to find a way to make it easier for all of us to see and believe it. Got it? Step up your game.

"This is more important than any of us."

Turning to Carly, he continued, "Now, dear, please go on."

"As you can see by these readings, I was far from asleep. It was like I was awake the whole time—vision upon vision and emotion upon emotion came over me. The feelings were intense and the physical sensations were incredible. I felt as if I were in the water swimming together with the whales. And by the way, that huge whale is, in fact, the oldest right whale. She showed me the truth about what this all means.

"All whales are born with knowledge that is passed down from their mothers, probably in the same way I get my visions, and that knowledge is about the end of this planet.

"Repeatedly, I have seen empty, dirty beaches and green, dark skies, and I've smelled the stench of death. And the latest visions were the sharpest and most troubling. The oceans were littered with dead fish, the water had turned black, and the air had become unbreathable. You see, even for the whales, the world is dying.

"John, when you look at a whale, what is the first thing you see in its eyes? Sadness, right? Tim, do you not see it as well? And Eleanor, I know you see it for sure. Even you, Captain, I know that you do, too. The whales are sad because they know that the end of the world is coming, and it is coming faster and faster because of us.

"As I said, all whales are born with this innate knowledge and also with the knowledge of their own deaths.

"Eleanor, you have studied enough whales in your time to know that they use so much more of their brain than humans do. Dolphins are believed to use as much as 85 percent of their brain while humans use just 10 percent.

"Whales have been around for many centuries, and their inherent knowledge of the end of the world has been passed down from generation to generation. And for many of those generations, they have searched for ways to warn us about the earth's impending doom.

"In the early days, knowing full well that they would be killed, these whales rose to the ocean's surface to sacrifice themselves in the hopes that in their final moments of life there would be a connection with the humans and that somewhere, somehow some human would hear and understand their warning."

By now Eleanor was trembling and John was entranced. Carly's words were so deliberate that everyone immediately realized that what she was saying was true, and they needed to know more.

After another sip of coffee, Carly continued, "That horrible childhood experience of witnessing a whale beach herself—you know, the experience that prompted me to become a marine biologist—well, that was that whale's attempt to make a connection with humans. However, I just didn't recognize it at the time, and neither did anyone else.

"John. Captain. Whales beach themselves when they are dying as a way to reach out to humans to make a connection.

"Do you hear me? For hundreds of years, whales have been trying to tell us what is coming, and we have been too deaf to hear their warnings.

"But because I was just a child then, I might have

been more receptive to "hearing" the message that that first whale was sending. And now being with Otis' mother during Otis' birth and then being with them before and during the shark attack, I heard Otis' mother's warning message more distinctly. My childhood connection happened again; but this time, it stuck for both of us. Do you hear me? It stuck for both of us!"

After another sip of coffee and getting no reaction from the others, Carly continued, "The Old Whale knew there was a connection. She knew that I was the one, but she was also afraid.

"Whales do not know or understand about our instruments and equipment. They do not know that we humans must first understand something before we believe it. For whales, it is just knowing and believing.

"The Old Whale's violent reaction was her way of trying to protect her species, which, at that moment, was more important to her than contacting us…or so she thought.

"When she came alongside later on, she got to know me and learn about all of you. It all became clear to her as well as to me. She awakened to the possibilities of finally changing things. Do you understand? In their dying, they have been trying to save us all."

By the time Carly had finished, she had tears in her eyes. She thought for sure someone would say that this was insane or stupid or that she was just a silly young girl. She expected it mainly from Eleanor; but no one said a word, not one word.

Then the silence was broken by a voice on the radio, "Guys, she's coming back."

CHAPTER 11

UNIT 6

The last one out the door, Eleanor grabbed the EEG unit and followed everyone topside.

As they gathered on the stern, Eleanor approached Carly. She had a much softer look on her face, an almost motherly look. "I am going with you," she said as she followed Carly down the ladder to the dive platform.

When Carly and Eleanor reached the platform, the whale that had once tried to sink Mother Earth rose to the surface. Eleanor's heart skipped a beat as the whale surfaced right beside her. She gazed into the whale's eyes and immediately realized that what Carly had described was all true; and she felt it, too.

As Carly reached out and patted the Old Whale, Otis appeared at the port side of the platform. Carly left the Old Whale and went to her little boy. She stretched out on the platform and stroked Otis just above his eye; and for little awhile, all seemed right with the world.

Eleanor was uncertain of what to do at first. Then, following Carly's example, she also lay down on the platform and touched the giant whale.

As she patted the whale, Eleanor realized that she had been wrong about so many things, and now she felt a rush of joy and the thrill of exploration that she had known as a young scientist. She no longer felt like the world-weary person that she had become. It was a wonderful moment.

Eleanor gently stroked the Old Whale a little bit more and then reached up to attach the EEG device to one of its callosities. Even though the whale fidgeted a little, Eleanor was able to successfully secure Unit 6 in place.

Although she did not have any visions or feel any strange sensations like Carly had, Eleanor did feel a connection to the whales. And with that, she realized that she was no longer Eleanor, but Ellie again, and it felt good.

In the meantime, Carly and Otis were having a blast sharing visions; and it was quite evident to the captain, John, and Tim. They could almost feel Otis' joy when he saw that Carly was safe. His new Mama was all right. And he even looked like he was smiling.

After spending a few more minutes with Otis and the Old Whale, the ladies stood up. Carly looked at Ellie and realized that Ellie was changed.

As the Old Whale swam away with Unit 6 attached, Otis let out a whopper of a water spout...all over Ellie! However, this time Ellie did not stew and stammer. This time she laughed aloud with delight.

After the ladies composed themselves, they headed up the ladder to join the others.

Captain Adare looked at Ellie and smiled, "You look happy, young lady!"

Ellie just nodded her head and gave him a big smile that was not about to fade any time soon. Perhaps this voyage had been better for her than she thought it would be.

John gave Carly a fatherly hug. And, as everyone stood looking at each other, Tim let out a laugh and yelled, "Oh, come on! Group hug!"

They all laughed and cheered, and even a few other crew members joined in the excitement.

CHAPTER 12

AROUND THE TIP

Morning came and Mother Earth was bursting with excitement again. With Carly's return and the Old Whale calmed down and understanding what was happening, the crew was much more relaxed and ready to see where this journey was taking them.

After breakfast, Tim headed into his cave (as he referred to it), a well-insulated, windowless room. Inside were all sorts of computer monitors. Some had the characteristic green sonar blips, others had multi-color displays, and one even had a video game on it. After all, if a guy's only job is to watch and listen to radio blips, then why not keep the reflexes active, too, was Tim's reasoning.

Tim was enjoying his morning coffee as he plotted the locations of all 35 whales. While Otis and the Old Whale were easy to pinpoint, the others were a little tricky, especially in a pod. But hey! This is what he was trained for; and in fairly short order, he had them all plotted on the map.

The pod was still about six miles ahead of Mother Earth and approaching the high-traffic waters of Miami, which could spell disaster for the slow-moving whales. So Tim reported his findings to Captain Adare who then notified the Coast Guard about the approaching whales.

The Coast Guard responded to Captain Adare with a Notice of Compliance stating that they will alert all incoming and outgoing ships about the whales' location and heading, and they would also dispatch several Coast Guard vessels to keep any intruding water craft at a safe distance.

Tim kept a watchful eye on the screens for any directional deviations by the whales, but none occurred; the whales steadfastly maintained their southerly heading.

Then Tim began pondering what Carly had told them all earlier—that whales know about the end of all life on earth and that we are the ones who hold the key, but the key *to what?*

Tim considered himself to be a pretty deep thinker, but even he found this hard to fathom. Nevertheless, after all he had seen on this trip, he could not deny that there definitely was some kind of communication going on between Carly and the whales.

Eventually, Tim's thoughts turned to what could possibly cause the end of the world. Could it be another giant asteroid, or perhaps a nuclear attack started by some unstable leader of a foreign country, or maybe climate change? Who knows? The whales know.

The more he thought about it, the more difficult it was for him to imagine the end of the world. The world couldn't die, could it? How would it happen? Would it be a long, slow, drawn-out process or would it all be gone in a flash?

And sailing on this ocean now, he could think only about how much life there was out there all around him. He couldn't even imagine there *not* being any life. He pointed at the monitor as if trying to show someone else the blips on the screen. Those blips are the whales! See? There *is* life out there! The world is not dying!

But the longer he watched those blips, the better he understood their message. These magnificent creatures that have been around for millions of years and that had once numbered in the thousands have since been reduced to a mere 35 in existence today.

Now Tim wondered how many other species have also been wiped out, so he decided to do some research on the Internet. He was shocked at the vastness of information that he found on the subject.

He discovered that nearly 500 different animal species had become extinct in the past 100 years alone because of hunting and loss of habitat. This is an alarming rate considering that approximately only 2 species per every 10,000 die off solely due to natural causes. The list of extinct species included the African Black Rhino, Bubal Hartebeest, Caribbean Monk Seal, Great Auk, Javan Tiger, Passenger Pigeon, Pyrenean Ibex, Quagga, Sea Mink, Tasmanian Tiger, and the Tecopa Pupfish just to name a few.

Tim was also alarmed to discover that close to 20,000 different species of plants, insects, fish, and other animals are on the verge of disappearing.

A tear came to his eye when he saw the picture of a giant softshell turtle whose species is now down to just four known survivors.

He realized that this was the fault of the human race. Humans had done this. Humans had accelerated all of this. For goodness sake! Forty percent of all of the species in North America alone have vanished!

Every day this planet was losing another form of life. Tim's mind began to spin at the math. He figured that at this rate, this much loss of wildlife may not be able to be halted. By the estimations stated on one website, the world could run out of life forms within the next 100 years. This is the approximate lifespan of people being born right now, so these folks could, in fact, be the final generation to walk the earth.

"Oh, Wow!" Tim said aloud to himself as he suddenly grasped the gravity of the situation. "What would happen to us? What would happen to humans? We would be extinct, too," was all he could think. "This is what the whales are trying to warn us about: *All* life on earth would cease to exist...*ALL* life."

When Tim's crewmate arrived to take over, Tim bolted out of the door full of all his newly acquired information. He needed to talk with Carly.

Carly had been sitting on the ship's bow all day recording every vision that came through her amazing mind. The things she learned from the visions were like nothing she could have imagined herself.

Every now and again, Otis took in a huge amount of air and then would see how deeply he could dive.

At those times, Carly could feel the sensation of the water pressure and see the beauty of the deep sea like no other human had ever seen it.

These visions ran like a movie in her mind, and as Otis swam deeper, Carly could see the coral reefs through his eyes. The crystal blue depths were incredibly astounding. All of the colors of the fish reminded her of just how extraordinary all of this life is. Just like the beautiful sunrises and the sky that is the Creator's canvass, the sea, too, was bursting with all colors imaginable. In every direction there was a yellow, a blue, a green, or a purple so dazzling that it was hard to believe that it all was real.

Carly had seen much of this as a diver, but never to the degree of clarity with which she witnessed it through the visions from Otis. It was through his eyes that she saw not only the vast array of colors, but also the sea life itself—from giant swarming masses of fish to the sea turtles swimming by. Life under the sea was bursting in all directions.

But just like the beautiful, colorful images that flashed through her mind, she occasionally saw an image that was colorless like a black and white photo with a lifeless, barren sea, and then the images would return to color again.

The visions that were devoid of life showed much more at times—things like places where dark expanses would appear in the water, thousands of tons of humans' trash completely covering the sea floor, and algae pools choking the oxygen from the water making it toxic. These were extremely troubling things for Carly to see, but she needed to see them. So Otis persisted in showing her.

Tim approached Carly slowly because he was always uncomfortable talking to women. He learned early on how to cover up his awkwardness by playing the clown and goof ball.

And although they had been working together for only a short time, he liked Carly very much. He thought she was beautiful, but felt that she was out of his league. Still, she had everything he wanted in a friend—she was smart, funny, pretty, and a little awkward, too. Plus she was *cool*...because he believed that she had a super power.

As he watched Carly writing in her notebook, something came over him, and he walked to her and said, "Hey!"

Startled, Carly looked up at Tim and giggled. He relaxed as she started to speak, "Tim, I cannot believe all that I am able to see through his eyes. It is all so beautiful, yet so tragic. The heartbreaking outcome for us all is the end of the world. You know that, don't you?"

"You took the words right out of my mouth. I have been doing some research, too, and it looks like the end may come sooner then we think.

"It is like the human race just hasn't cared about or has not been completely aware of the massively destructive impact it has been having on the planet and other creatures for centuries. And the end may be accelerated as more creatures become extinct," was Tim's sad reply.

Carly looked at him, "I think you may be right. I told you that I learned that each whale already knows the time of its own death. And while Otis has not shared his "end time" with me, I do know that he is here to witness the end of all life. The average right whale lives to be around 100 years old. So, the end could potentially happen *not* within *our* lifetime, but within the lifetimes of *our children*."

Tim liked the sound of that last statement—the sound of "our children." So, he took a deep breath, hugged her, and asked, "Would you like to go out with me at the next port?"

And just as he got the words out, a giant splash hit them both! It seems that when you share a mind connection with a whale, nothing is secret; and Otis decided to cool off the current state of affairs a bit. Otis' shenanigans were starting to take its toll on the wardrobes of many.

As they headed inside to change out of their drenched clothes, Tim told Carly all about what he had learned about the animals dying off at the hands of humans. He explained how this phenomenon has accelerated to a point where the ability to reverse the situation has become nearly impossible unless some drastic measures are taken.

Carly liked Tim, but she was still a little nervous herself. Yet, as he talked about all that he had learned, she could not help but reach out and take his hand.

Delighted, all Tim could do was smile, and he almost skipped, too. But instead, he just did a double step. Then he and Carly laughed together as they walked through the hallway.

CHAPTER 13

ELLIE'S GREAT REVEAL

Rounding the tip of Florida, Mother Earth followed the whales through the Florida Keys and into the Gulf of Mexico. Meanwhile, Ellie was busy capturing EEG data from Carly, Otis, and the Old Whale.

When they weren't working, Tim and Carly spent a good deal of time together. They often sat on the deck and played with Otis who had learned to trust Tim. Carly had reassured Otis that Tim was a good guy and that Otis had no reason to question his "mother" after all.

John spent most of his days going back and forth between studies with Ellie and studying the route the whales were heading.

John liked spending time with Ellie. He found it both enjoyable and fascinating to watch her work.

He saw how she now struggled less with the way things once had been for her. He noticed that out here on the ocean, Ellie was learning to be her old self again, and how after a few weeks at sea, she seemed to relax more easily. She even wore her hair down all the time now, and John admired how her hair accentuated her perfect Irish jaw line.

John and Ellie were research colleagues, and John did not want to cross the fine line from coworkers to companions like Carly and Tim had done. However, the thought of Carly and Tim being together actually made John smile.

Captain Adare walked into the galley for the daily briefing. "It is great to see you all smiling! No whales are attacking. Otis is enjoying swimming along with us. And love is in the air!"

He nodded towards Tim and Carly who both blushed. And then he nodded at John and Ellie, but they stepped away from each other and shook their heads; however, Ellie smiled at the notion. The sea really did do her well, she thought.

The captain continued, "I have no idea of what our final destination will be; however, we are still following the whales, and they are presently about six miles ahead of us and traveling through the Florida Keys heading toward the Gulf.

"We will be stopping briefly in Islamorada to pick up some new equipment that John and Ellie have requested. While in port, we also will be taking on a new passenger, a non-marine scientist. John, would you please explain."

John stepped up and proceeded, "As you know, Ellie has been monitoring the EEG readings from Carly, Otis, and the Old Whale. And we have some good news about that—great news, actually.

"The monitoring devices that we reconfigured to fit the whales have been a huge success. We can see the visions that Carly receives from the whales...well, sort of see them. We can interpret the readings, but we need to convert our findings to concrete evidence that we can show to the world. Right now it is just our word and a whole lot of assumptions." Then he turned the meeting over to Ellie.

Ellie showed everyone the stack of papers that she had been studying. She pulled out one page in particular and passed it around explaining that it was an article about researchers at the University of California, Berkeley, whose ground-breaking work, which culminated in September 2011, described the capability of making computer-generated images from a person's visions and thoughts.

The images were not very clear back then, but are quite remarkable now thanks to the technological advancements that have been made since then. Those scientists had tried it on animals, and they had tried it on humans, but they never tried it in a shared-vision, multiple-species scenario.

Ellie continued to explain how this technology may hold the key to everything they had been witnessing on this trip.

With this equipment, they could distinguish between a vision that was shared and one that was not. By analyzing Carly's and Otis' EEG readings and demonstrating that they were sharing the same images, they would be able to prove that this is authentic indeed.

Everyone was excited by the news, and their minds raced with possibilities of what it would mean to have had the opportunity to be a part of history—a very big part—if they saved the world.

Ellie continued, "Do you all understand what this means? And from the look on your faces, I think that you do. It means that Otis' mother did not die in vain and that our journey here has a higher purpose.

Right now the planet on which we live is dying. We humans would like to believe that the world will live on forever; however, humanity has become indifferent to the consequences of its actions, which, sadly, has perpetuated the earth's demise."

Tim enthusiastically added his two cents, "Otis will live to be nearly 100 years old. He has the visions in his head and sees the end of life. We have to act!"

He looked around and saw that everyone was staring at him. Then he realized that they already felt the same way, too.

Ellie's response was a simple, "Yes, Tim."

She *had* changed. At one time, she would have made some sort of belittling reply, but now she just smiled and laughed at his enthusiasm.

Ellie continued, "Bryce Bolton will be joining us at the next port. He is a young scientist who is rather well-connected. His father is a senator, and so this may be exactly what the right whales need to get their message out.

"I haven't met him personally, but we have spoken on the phone several times. He is aware of the nature of some of the visions that Carly and Otis have shared, but he needs to know about it all just like everyone does."

Then the captain concluded the meeting saying, "Carly dear, I think you are going to feel even more like a lab rat pretty soon. Please make Otis comfortable with what is to come.

"Dismissed."

CHAPTER 14

ISLAMORADA

Known as the *Key for the Well-To-Do*, Islamorada is a place all its own. Even when the wealthy come here, they find it easy to relax and unwind. And that is just what the crew of the Mother Earth needed after several weeks at sea—rest and relaxation.

Mother Earth followed the whales, but this route into the Gulf was very odd. Right whales never head this far into the Gulf; they normally head past Cuba and into the warmer southern waters. But then again, nothing about this journey has been normal.

The whales realized that Mother Earth was heading into port and positioned themselves a few miles away in deeper waters to feed. Even Otis went to join them. Carly actually felt comforted knowing that Otis was going to be with his own kind for a while because she, too, needed to be with her own kind for a while.

As the Mother Earth pulled alongside the dock and the mooring lines were tied off, the crew disembarked as quickly as possible. Ellie met John, Tim, the captain, and Carly on deck and insisted they would not be drinking beer and Tequila as they had done at the last port. She had no desire to experience a repeat of the awful after-effects of that soirée.

As she turned to Carly, Ellie smiled in amusement. Perplexed by Ellie's amused gaze, Carly responded with a puzzled, "What?"

Then the captain, Tim, and John also noticed it, and they began to chuckle.

Carly stammered, "What? What? What?"

"Honey, you won't need this for now," replied Ellie as she lifted the monitoring device off of Carly's head.

And Carly started laughing with everyone else. "No. I guess I won't. So, where is this guy who is going to look inside my head?"

And just as she had said that, a tall, tanned, handsome man started waving and yelling, "Hello! Hello!" from across the dock.

As he got closer, both Carly and Ellie smiled as the scent of his cologne wafted passed them.

The newcomer requested permission to come aboard, and, of course, Captain Adare granted his request.

He introduced himself as Bryce and began shaking hands with everyone. And with each handshake, he repeated his name as if to make certain that everyone knew who he was.

John and Tim immediately decided that they didn't like this new guy. And even Captain Adare welcomed him in an unusually reserved manner. However, the ladies seemed slightly smitten with him.

Bryce waved and shouted to a group of men who were pulling equipment-filled carts down the pier toward Mother Earth, "Hurry up, you slow pokes! They're not that heavy. Hurry up!"

It sounded like he was scolding them, which made Carly and Ellie rethink their original feelings a bit.

As the men approached, Bryce started barking orders as if he were the captain.

And that is when the captain interrupted, "Bryce, we don't talk like that to the workers here. They help us. And because they help us, we don't have any problems. So, please watch how you speak to them."

Bryce turned to the captain, "Captain, with all due respect, they are here to help me, and I will…"

The captain raised his hand to silence Bryce, "I am not one to be addressed in that manner. While you are aboard the Mother Earth, you will pay attention to and respect what I say, no questions asked. Understood?"

Bryce stopped immediately, and the workers finished hauling the equipment aboard.

John asked Tim to show the dock hands where to put everything, and Tim took them down into the cabin area. As they disappeared below decks, another individual walked up the gang plank, except this person did not ask permission to come aboard.

Bryce hurriedly brushed past the captain as he extended his hand to the older gentleman, "Hello, Dad!"

And this is all that John, Carly, and Ellie had heard.

However, Captain Adare heard nothing as he turned and asked, "You do know that it is common courtesy to request permission to come aboard a vessel, don't you?" as he extended his hand to the rather rotund man.

Then Captain Adare turned to the others and introduced the visitor, "Everyone, please meet the senator from these parts. This is Bryce's father, Senator Darin Bolton."

Everyone greeted the senator with a polite, "How do you do?" However, they were all reluctant to shake hands with him.

The senator wore an ill-fitting, sweat-stained, white silk suit; a red, white, and blue tie; and an American flag pin on his lapel as if trying to convince people that he loved America. However, his appearance was not very convincing.

After the introductions had been made, the senator attempted to make a joke about the heat being oppressive, but it was barely 85 degrees and everyone was rather comfortable.

Then the senator surveyed the group, pointed a stubby finger towards Carly, and continued, "You must be the young lady who my son told me about—the one who thinks she can see visions and communicate with the whales. I hear that it has something to do with pollution, or the end of life on this planet, or some other kind of complete nonsense.

"Well, being the head of the Senate Appropriations Committee on Climate Change, I can assure you there are no such issues. Almost all of that research is nothing more than hooey made up by..."

"Made up by people like those you are addressing right now, Senator?" Ellie retorted. Her face was as red as her hair, and she began to think that perhaps she had made a major mistake in contacting this Bryce character.

The Senator interrupted her, "Miss, I do apologize. Where are my manners? You are right. And to make it up to you all, I would like to take everyone to lunch at the yacht club today."

"That won't be necessary, Senator. It is extremely pricey there," Captain Adare responded.

The senator looked at the captain, "Don't worry, Captain. The taxpayers are paying for it. And if it gets too expensive, I will just cut another handout program." But he did not say it jokingly.

And with that, everyone followed Bryce and the senator down the gang plank and to the restaurant.

Carly's phone chimed as they walked into the building, and then she explained, "We will need an extra seat; someone else will be joining us shortly." Annoyed, the senator shook his head as he informed the hostess.

As everyone was ordering drinks, a spirited voice came from behind the table. "Is that my beautiful daughter! Oh my goodness! It is!"

Carly sank a few inches in her seat before standing and turning to greet her mother who raced past several tables to get to Carly and embrace her in a big hug! Carly had softened to receiving these hugs since having Otis in her life. Maybe Carly was beginning to understand what the parent-child connection was about after all.

Then Carly introduced her mother, "Everyone, this is my mother, Tina." All of the men stood to greet her, except the senator.

Tina was a lovely woman with flowing blonde hair and a shapely figure, and she seemed to glide as she walked. She had blue eyes, and she always seemed to be smiling. She was no stranger at meeting strangers, immediately making them feel relaxed and welcomed. Carly always felt a little intimidated by her mother's natural charm and beauty. Tina's calm demeanor was a little unnerving at first, and that could be seen in the senator's face as he waited impatiently for everyone to finish meeting her.

It was obvious that Captain Adare was taken by her. He leaned in as they shook hands and whispered, "It is my pleasure to meet such a lovely woman and the creator of such a gifted creature as our dear Carly."

Tina gently placed her hand on the captain's cheek, "Oh! What a nice thing to say. Thank you."

As everyone took their seats, Bryce looked at his father and asked him if he was going to introduce himself.

Senator Bolton scoffed, "I already know this woman, and she knows me! She has been a thorn in my side for decades now, always trying to limit some form of emissions from my many donors' companies here in the area. Had I known that she would be here, I would not have made these arrangements."

As she took her seat next to the Captain, Tina smiled at the Senator and said, "Oh, Senator! You say the nicest things. I am merely here to see my daughter whom I have not seen in ages because I have been a little too busy trying to stop people like you from destroying this beautiful ecosystem.

"So for civility's sake, let's enjoy our lunch and see if your son can actually prove that the whales *are* trying to tell my daughter something about the end of the world that may be happening just because of people like you." And she said it all with a smile.

And it was clear to everyone at the table that Tina was a force to be reckoned with. Even Ellie clenched her fist under the table and silently agreed, "Yeah!"

John was stunned. And Tim whispered to Carly, "You didn't tell me I was going to meet your family." Carly smiled understandingly at Tim. She was her mother's daughter after all.

As the small talk finally dwindled, the senator asked, "So, what is this all about?

"They say you talk to whales. Does that mean you can understand all their squeaks and squeels? And when you talk to them, do you do it in their form of speech?

"Come on, young lady, share some squeaks and squeels with us!" He said it with a cynical smile, trying to be humorous and condescending at the same time. But no one laughed.

Carly stared at the senator. She made a few clicking sounds and squeels, and then she ended with a deep moan.

"*Good!* young lady. What did you just say?"

Carly stood up, stepped back from the table, and replied, "I called you an asshole!"

Then she abruptly turned and left the room. John spit his coffee across the table, some of which landed on the senator's white silk suit.

Captain Adare burst out laughing, while Tina and Ellie exclaimed, "*Brava!*"

Bryce looked at his dad and pleaded, "Dad! Really? I have to work with these people. Could you please stop!"

Tim ran after Carly.

A few moments later, Ellie picked up the conversation. "There *is* something going on here.

"There are equivalent EEG readings during these moments of shared visions, and as far as we can currently tell, Carly's descriptions of her visions are accurate. However, we need to determine if the visions are shared; and if they are, we must listen to what the whales are saying."

Tina added, "Senator, although we greatly disagree about the extent to which mankind has negatively impacted the Earth, it is imperative to learn whether we are or are not the definitive cause of the earth's demise. Therefore, if the whales are trying to tell us something, we all do need to listen! And that includes you!"

Senator Bolton looked at them and declared, "Whales don't pay for my reelection, unless it is on the deck of a whaling ship. Bryce, you know what to do." Then he stood up, paid the bill, and walked away.

John and Captain Adare looked at Bryce and asked, "What did he mean by that?"

"My father pays for my research, and I will report to him as well as to you. But I promise to be fair and open-minded and to do my job properly. Just be aware that I tell my father everything."

"Oh! We will remember, all right!" they replied.

As they all headed back to the ship to get things in order, Tina walked with the captain.

It was obvious that the captain was attracted to her. Tina had been a solid part of the area for over a decade, and the captain was familiar with her work, but he had no idea that she was Carly's mother. Small world, he thought.

As they walked along, Tina explained that she and Carly's father had never officially divorced.

While he had loved to fish and was happy being on the Georgia coast, Tina wasn't. For all of her life, she had a calling to speak up for the animals of this world that could not speak up for themselves, so she was always traveling from place to place.

For most of Carly's early years, Tina had traveled. But when Carly's father passed away shortly after Carly started at the University of Miami, Tina returned to the area to protest the sugar cane industry's pollution of the water ways. That is what placed her at direct odds with Senator Bolton—his campaign is almost entirely funded by the sugar cane industry.

Over the past few years Tina had been struggling with how to be in her daughter's life. She didn't know if or how much Carly wanted her mother involved. But when Carly called and told her about the son of the senator coming aboard, Tina knew that she needed to step in to make sure that Carly's amazing gift did not get twisted.

Gently grasping the captain's arm, Tina asked, "May I please come along?"

And without hesitation, Captain Adare nodded in agreement as if charmed by an angel.

As they strolled along the cobble stone streets of Islamorada's tourist area and eventually down to the beautiful white-sand beach, they got to know each other quite well. Sharing tales of their travels and all the wonders of the world they had experienced, the captain found it refreshing to meet a kindred spirit, especially one filled with so much love for the earth.

Before long they came upon Carly and Tim. Tina hugged her daughter again and whispered, "Now, kiddo, *that* was epic!"

As the four friends talked and laughed while they walked along the beach, the sun began to set on the horizon. They each marveled at its grandeur, the beauty of which cannot be put into words. Every color of the spectrum is in a Florida Keys sunset, and this one was no exception.

When the sun sank below the horizon, they went to a small Tiki bar and kept the conversations going.

Tina learned all about the death of Otis' mother and how the ship had been rammed by the Old Whale, which all seemed surreal to Tina.

Then Tina announced that she would be joining the crew, and Carly was glad to hear that. Finally, she was going to have her mother around; and, honestly, she needed that right now.

Back aboard the Mother Earth, Ellie and John were getting Bryce and his gear situated. While his machines were being installed, he explained that monitors would need to be placed on both Carly and Otis and that they would need to stay in very close proximity of them in order to get accurate readings. Then during Bryce's explanations, a little bit of Eleanor returned, which caught John off guard.

"Bryce, your father would hate to see these visions be a reality. His entire career has been funded by the companies that are killing our planet. If I find out that you have tainted any of our research, even in the slightest, you will become chum for the sharks. *Get it?*"

"Eleanor, I am a scientist just like you, and I am here to see that the truth gets told. But I still have to inform my father. And, yes, I *get it*."

John never said a word during the exchange, but he was definitely amused.

CHAPTER 15

VISIONS COME TO LIFE

The next morning the Mother Earth was buzzing with activity. With the addition of the two new crew members and a ton of new equipment, Mother Earth seemed to be bursting at her seams, and everyone was scrambling everywhere. But one thing about a crew, it was like family.

As Carly, John, Tim, Ellie, and Tina were having breakfast, Bryce came in with his tray and a huge smile. Then as he was about to sit down, Ellie got up, despite not finishing her meal. Apparently, the disagreement from the night before was still fresh on her mind.

Bryce stopped her. He apologized profusely and asked her to stay. Ellie sat down, but it was obvious that she still was not happy. The exchange was not lost on the others either.

This was prime time for Tim to say, "Well, it seems that we are off to an awkward start. That's about normal around here!" And everyone laughed.

After some small talk, Bryce explained that he was ready to calibrate his equipment and that he would like to begin with Carly's monitor. Carly nodded. By now she *was* starting to feel like one of those lab rats she used to work with in college.

Bryce went on to explain that he would be modifying Carly's head set so that he could monitor her brain waves, and then he would do the same with Otis' monitors.

Carly gladly handed over her head gear. Then she finished her breakfast and headed outside to be with Otis.

When everyone else finished their breakfasts, they all went about their duties, all except for Tina who went to check on her daughter.

John, Ellie, and Bryce headed to the lab to work on the equipment, and Tim headed to the sonar room to track the whales for a while and to talk with Captain Adare.

As Tina walked out onto the deck, she saw Otis swimming at less than an arms length from where Carly had her hand extended so she could touch him. Carly was conversing with Otis as easily as she would with another person, except Otis was a whale. And then Carly brushed her hand above his eye as he stared into her face.

The gentleness of this massive creature amazed Tina. In just a few short weeks, Otis had grown to about 20 feet long and really started looking more and more like the other right whales in the pod; that is, except for those ugly boxes attached to his head.

She realized that her mother was watching, and Carly sat up immediately.

Tina said, "Oh, dear, just relax. It is beautiful to watch. What were you two discussing?" Then she sat down next to them.

"I was telling Otis about how we are going to make our visions come to life and that I didn't trust Bryce to do the right thing. That's all."

Tina agreed, "I don't trust him either. The apple usually doesn't fall far from the tree, and his father, the senator, is a real piece of work."

Tina laid her hand on Otis for the first time, and continued, "But, darlings, the truth always has a way of coming out. This has all happened for a reason. And you two were specifically chosen to share what the whales have been trying to tell us for generations."

"Mom, we know."

Just then the Old Whale quietly surfaced near them, and Carly continued, "The Old Whale wants to tell you something."

Tina stared in awe at Carly and then at the whales.

"Mom, she says we all will need your strength…and soon. Just do not waiver. She will be with you."

At that moment Captain Adare's voice came over the loudspeaker asking everyone to assemble on deck.

As everyone gathered, the captain began, "Thank you all for coming so quickly.

"It looks like the whales are now heading up the Gulf-side of the Florida coast toward an area known as the Dead Coast.

"It is called this not because of ship wrecks or missing planes, but because the water in this vicinity has become poisonous to sea creatures.

"The runoff from the sugar cane fields, factories, agricultural fertilizers, and pesticides dumps right into this portion of the gulf. The water here has become toxic, so toxic, in fact, that this area is now completely devoid of all water-born creatures.

"It also has become the resting area to several massive top-side oil spills over the years. Many of you may have heard of that big oil company's rig whose drill broke and spilled millions of gallons of crude oil into the gulf.

"Well, the tides have never been able to completely defuse that spill; instead, that oil spill mushroomed throughout this portion of the gulf, choking off all life.

"Because of that and other spills and the many decades of other toxic chemicals being dumped into the gulf in the name of money, sea life in this region is now non-existent; hence, the term Dead Coast.

"After talking with John and Tim a little while ago, we came to the conclusion that if the whales have something to show us, as Carly has described in her visions, then this may be the place *where* they will show us.

"Everyone should keep in mind that this water *is* toxic, and we will be reaching the first dead zone in just a few days. I will let you know when we are close.

"It is more important than ever that we work together. Everyone should assist Bryce in any way that he needs you."

Bryce waved his hand and asked the captain if they could meet in private. The captain's response surprised Bryce.

"No! We cannot. Anything you have to say can be said right here!"

Bryce stammered for a second, "All right. Well, let's just say this is all true, which I highly doubt. But, let's just *say* it is true. Why would the whales want to show us this particular area when we already know about it?"

The captain smiled at Bryce, "You are right, Bryce. *We* all know about it. *We* are involved in the world of marine study.

"But, and I'm saying this in all seriousness, it is because of people like your father, the senator, that most of the world *doesn't* know anything about it.

"So, yes, young man, we can talk in private in a few minutes.

"And Tina and John, please join us.

"Dismissed."

As the crew dispersed and returned to their duties, Tina joined John and Bryce as they headed down the hallway to the captain's office. As they turned the corner to knock on the captain's door, Carly, Tim, and Ellie met them.

The captain opened the door, "This was supposed to just be the four of us, but you three should hear this as well. Come in.

"I have something very important to tell you, so please don't interrupt me. Hold your questions until I'm all finished. All right?"

Everyone nodded in agreement.

"Bryce, I received an email today from your father's office. It arrived as we started heading up the

Gulf. And John, I know you received an email from the university as well. I was copied on that one, and that's how I know about it. You all can relax. I'm not reading everyone's email.

"Bryce, the one from your father was clear: No marine studies by outside organizations are to be made in these areas.

"He states that privately funded groups have already cleared these areas as safe and just fine, which *we* all know is a lie.

"Anyway, he goes on to say that any non-licensed commercial vessel in these waters will be stopped, boarded, and possibly impounded by the Coast Guard.

"So, with that being said, Ellie and Bryce, how far away from Otis can we be and still continue to receive a clear signal from his monitors?

"Wait. Before you answer that, first let me tell you about the email from the university. John, I'm sure you have read it.

"That email basically states that *if* John and his team do not abandon this expedition, all funding for it will be pulled. And we have been given 72 hours to start packing it up."

Tina responded first, "Bryce, it sounds like your daddy is playing some games with the university and its federal funding."

The captain looked at Tina, "Please, we don't need that right now."

"Ellie, how far away can we be?" the captain asked again.

"One mile, Captain. One mile is the farthest distance away that Otis can be," she replied.

Tim chimed in, "Captain, based on the whales' present course, one mile would put us all within the toxic plumes."

"I know," replied the captain.

Bryce smirked, and maybe Carly was the only one who noticed it.

The captain continued, "John, Ellie, and Bryce, get on it! Get me as much distance as I can have.

"Tim, keep setting things up.

"Carly and Tina, you go to Otis and let him know what might be coming and assure him that we are not going anywhere. We will be with him all the way!"

Bryce chimed in, "Captain, I know my father. He follows through on what he says. You don't want to lose Mother Earth, do you?"

"Don't worry. I won't lose the Mother Earth," the captain declared. "*You* just make sure that we can see the visions from Carly and Otis, *and* you make sure those visions come *alive*. We have only 72 hours, guys. Now, *get moving!*"

"Dismissed."

CHAPTER 16

THE DEAD COAST

Everyone returned to their stations—the captain to his bridge; Tim to the sonar room; John, Ellie, and Bryce to the lab; and Carly and Tina to the ship's stern so that Carly could talk with Otis.

"I'm so proud of you, kiddo. You discovered that you have a remarkable gift, and then you received that incredible knowledge from the whales. And through it all, you have not faltered," Tina said as she gripped her daughter's hand.

As they walked along, Tina added, "Sweetheart, I know that you are scared, and I know that you may even feel a little threatened. And I can imagine that's how the whales have felt for their entire existence, but they will be here to thrive and grow, and you will, too.

"I knew that awful senator was going to be a jerk, but don't any of you worry. I have a little something in the works, and it's not just me in on it, either. Trust me. All will be OK. Now go tell Otis what is going on." And then she kissed Carly on the cheek.

"I've already told him," replied Carly as she tapped on her temple.

Meanwhile, John, Ellie, and Bryce started reconfiguring the transmitters for both Carly and Otis so that their devices would be able to transmit their visions to Bryce's equipment.

As Bryce explained it, in early experiments using these devices, only still images—like photographs—could be transmitted. This new equipment should, in theory, allow them to see through both Carly's and Otis' eyes as well as through their minds' eyes, capturing their visions and thoughts as if watching a television show.

Ellie was a little awestruck at this idea. As she worked, she couldn't help but think of all the applications where this could help—perhaps helping people overcome emotional blocks or maybe even assisting witnesses in identifying criminals. The applications seemed endless, she thought. This could all be so amazing.

John, on the other hand, didn't care about any other applications. He concentrated solely on strengthening this booster-system signal as much as possible.

They needed to be outside of the Dead Coast zone or they actually could lose everything—the crew could go to jail, the captain could lose Mother Earth, and John's job at the university would be over; not to mention that if Carly and Otis were right, the fate of every living thing on the planet could be at stake.

Within a few hours, Bryce turned to John and Ellie and announced, "I think we are done. It looks like these units are ready."

Carly's headgear didn't look much different except for the two larger boxes attached to the head strap; however, Otis' unit looked huge in comparison to the little black boxes he was currently wearing.

Bryce explained, "This one unit for Otis replaces all of those other units. It houses everything we will need and is only 12 inches high by 18 inches long, so it's not really too big."

John and Ellie laughed a little as Bryce said that with a straight face because to them, Otis' gear looked huge.

"John, please take these to Carly and Otis and explain the process while I calibrate the receiving equipment. I brought two units just in case there was a failure with one of them," he said as he pointed to a large chest on the floor.

"Also, make sure Carly thinks clearly and that she asks Otis to do the same. After the images start coming through, tell her to envision a flower followed by Otis envisioning the same flower. Then they should follow that pattern envisioning a plane, and then a turtle. If they both can do that, then it proves they are communicating on a much higher level. But folks, please understand that you all might be disappointed."

"No, we won't," John remarked as he left the lab.

A few minutes later, Tina walked in. "I came in to see the visions come to life. Bryce, do you mind?"

"Of course not. But as I just told John, you might be disappointed."

When John reached Carly and Otis, he explained Bryce's instructions while he fastened Carly's head gear on her, and then he radioed the captain to bring Mother Earth to a stop. Captain Adare stopped the engines, and both the Mother Earth and Otis slowly came to a stop side by side.

John reached across Otis and started removing the existing units while Carly patted Otis reassuringly and said, "It's all right, little one. It will be over soon."

Once all of the old units were removed and the new single unit was attached to Otis, John radioed to Bryce to switch on the monitors.

Ellie, Tina, and Bryce stared at the monitor that was synchronized to Carly's head gear. Tina also watched Bryce intently, keeping a close eye on everything he was doing. Then slowly, very slowly, an image of what Carly was seeing began to appear on the screen. It wasn't quite like watching television, but it was obvious that they were seeing precisely what Carly was seeing.

Bryce made a few adjustments to the machine, and then an image of a sunflower appeared. "What is that?" Tina asked.

"It's a sunflower. Let me tell you how this works.

When I flip this switch—here on the board—the image changed from what Carly was *seeing* to what she was *thinking*," Bryce explained as he pointed to a toggle switch on what looked like a recording studio's mixing board.

"I instructed Carly to concentrate on a flower. Now let's turn to Otis' monitor and see if this works."

Bryce switched on Otis' monitor screen, and within moments, a blurry image appeared. Bryce made some adjustments, turning knobs to the left and to the right. All the while, Tina watched him closely.

As the image on the screen became sharper, they saw the back of the Mother Earth from a water-surface point of view, and then they saw an image of John and Carly coming into focus.

Ellie let out a slight gasp as she realized that they were watching the world through Otis' eyes.

Then Bryce threw the toggle switch, and all three gasped as the identical image of Carly's sunflower appeared on Otis' monitor, too. This was quickly followed by an image of a plane and then by a sea turtle. This confirmed that Carly and Otis were definitely communicating with each other by way of their thoughts.

Ellie grabbed the radio from Bryce, hit the all-channel button, and yelled into it, "Oh! My God! It worked! Carly and Otis *can* talk to each other!"

Even down in the lab, they could hear cheering from everyone aboard Mother Earth.

Shortly thereafter, Tim joined John and Carly on the stern and watched Carly intently staring into Otis' eyes.

John whispered to Tim, "Did the captain talk with you? Are you ready?"

Tim nodded.

As the seconds ticked by, the images switched from shared images to ones that seemed to be in real time. They quickly learned how to tell the difference: A shared vision would first appear on one screen and then appear on the second screen a few seconds later. But when it was not a shared vision, different scenes appeared on each monitor screen.

Ellie simply could not believe this. At first all she could think was, "Wow!" Her second thought was about how they could market this, but she quickly shook off that thought and kept watching the screens.

Tina, on the other hand, was the first to notice that Otis started to share a vision, "Look! It must be the vision that had upset Carly so much. It must be what the whales have been trying to tell us as Carly had said."

Otis' vision was of an ocean that was very full of life. There were fish of all colors, shapes, and sizes darting this way and that. The water was beautiful and clear. And as Otis surfaced, they could see the shore. The sky was a beautiful blue, and there was abundant life everywhere.

Then the image returned to the sea. But this time it was different, much different. The water was changing. It was no longer crystal clear; instead, it was black or dark green in areas. There were no fish or other sea creatures. Trails of pollutants were visible. There were swirls of chemicals, trails of oil, and garbage was piled everywhere. And as the vision turned towards the beach again, nothing was alive there anymore. Strewn throughout the area were skeletons and garbage as far as the eye could see. Even the sky had become a greenish-grey and blocked the sun. There was nothing left alive on the land or in the sea.

After that vision faded from both monitors, another one appeared on Carly's monitor first (meaning that Carly had initiated it).

This vision was similar to the one from Otis, but Carly's showed things to be not nearly as bad. It showed the world as it is now—there was some pollution, but not as much life as there once had been. However, the skies were clear, and there were animals and people on the shore.

Tina was the first to point out to the others that this must be how they talk—one shows the other something, and then it goes back and forth like a conversation.

Everyone watched and eagerly anticipated what might appear next, and they didn't have to wait long. A real-time vision from Otis began coming in loud and clear.

Otis was at the surface, and on Carly's monitor screen, they watched as Carly and Otis looked at each other. Then Otis dove below the surface.

As he swam deeper, the water became shadowy. There was some life and a few fish here and there, but soon the water turned murky, and garbage was floating all around.

Farther on, he swam through an area that had a metallic rainbow-like shimmer, which had been caused by chemicals that had never dissipated.

As he swam deeper still, the water became jet black from oil spills of ages past, and there were no signs of life anywhere. Then Otis' monitor screen suddenly went blank.

He had swum far enough away from Mother Earth that his monitor's signal had been lost. Also, he was getting pretty close to the Dead Coast.

"That proves it, Bryce!" Tina exclaimed. "Your father, Senator Darrin *Bolemo* is *lying* about the environmental conditions in the Dead Coast!"

"*You're* wrong. And it is Senator *Bolton*," Bryce retorted.

"I prefer *Bolemo*; it's more fitting" Tina replied as she walked out. And Ellie followed.

As Tina and Ellie left the room, Bryce picked up his phone and sent a text: "Dad, you were right. The truth about the Dead Coast is about to come out."

"Relax, boy. The shrimp boats are already on their way," was the senator's reply.

CHAPTER 17

SHRIMP BOATS

As the news of the visions reached Captain Adare, he felt it was time to have another meeting. He radioed everyone to meet in the lab. And just as the captain walked in, he caught Bryce putting away his cell phone.

"Let me guess, Bryce. You called your father to tell him the great news."

Bryce nervously responded, "Yes, sir. And he was glad to hear it, too."

"Well, was he so glad as to allow us to travel into the Dead Coast?"

"Um, sir, I seriously doubt that will happen."

Just then everyone else came rushing into the room, and Captain Adare started the meeting, "I take it that we were not able to extend the signal range of Otis' monitor?"

"No," replied Ellie.

The captain continued, "So, then, here is our current situation: The Dead Coast extends roughly about two miles out from the shoreline, and the whales have entered the area already. However, I will not break any laws to do this, and I don't have the right to jeopardize any of your lives, plus I have no desire to lose Mother Earth. So, for now we are going to stay as close to the border as safely possible and collect all the data and visions from Carly and Otis that we can. Since this ship is a commercial vessel, we cannot enter that region without permission from the senator's office; and, quite frankly, I don't think we will get that right now."

Bryce seemed to smile at the captain's last comment while there were some under-the-breath mumblings from the others.

Then a voice came from Tim's radio and broke the air of disappointment as one of the sonar techs reported, "Tim, there are several large boat signatures heading towards the whales' location—possibly shrimp boats or some other large fishing boats.

"And Tim, there is also one *huge* vessel heading our way...and fast. It should reach us within two hours. It looks like a Coast Guard cutter!"

Upon hearing this news, the captain radioed the bridge, "Kick it up a notch! Keep us out of the Dead Coast, but give us distance and time!"

Everyone was a bit concerned by the technician's report; but the captain, John, Tim, Tina were not really surprised.

Carly, however, was shaking. She was furious and turning red. She looked squarely at Bryce and snapped, "They had better *be* shrimp boats!"

And as she ran out of the room, a vision suddenly appeared on her monitor—a vision of Carly punching Bryce. Tim smiled, but Bryce just brushed it off.

The captain looked at everyone and ordered, *"Come on! Let's move!*

"Bryce! Set that contraption to record everything, and then come to the bridge with me." Then the captain winked in John's direction.

John reached the stern of Mother Earth first and saw something that he had not expected. Carly had taken the launch and was speeding away alone towards the whales. The captain radioed to John, "I know. I see her. Just stick to what I told you."

Ellie looked at John and asked, "What is she doing?"

"She is doing what any mother would do to protect her baby," he replied.

Ellie never had children of her own, and she still struggled inside with being Eleanor. She still wrestled with being a "good" person and understanding everything that that entails versus fighting to be accepted for "things and accomplishments."

Watching Carly run off now to do the right thing, despite the consequences, helped Ellie to understand it all a little better: If one must compromise one's morals in order to be accepted by certain people, then one is being accepted by the wrong kind of people.

She shouted, *"Go, Carly! Go!"*

Bryce joined the captain on the bridge.

Captain Adare greeted Bryce and invited him to stand beside him, "Bryce, do you know why those boats are heading towards the whales? Do you know why there is a Coast Guard vessel heading my way, even though I have broken no laws? Think carefully before you respond, boy."

Bryce wondered why everyone kept calling him "boy." He often thought it was because he followed the crowd instead of leading it. In his heart he really wanted to be a leader; however, living under his cantankerous, domineering father, he was never allowed to lead. He knew only how to follow.

Like so many others knew that Bryce would never be a leader, Bryce knew it now, too. He would be merely a follower and a boy in the eyes of real men.

Nevertheless, that realization did not stop him from looking squarely into the captain's eyes and lying, "No, sir. I have no idea."

The captain smiled wryly, "I was hoping you would say that."

He pointed to a small speed boat approaching Mother Earth and brought Mother Earth to a stop so that the other boat could come alongside and tie off.

"Should I go down there, Captain?

"No, Bryce. I want you right here. I want you here where you can watch all of this unfold, boy."

As Bryce watched from the bridge, he saw several men with computers, a satellite-dish, and cameras come aboard Mother Earth and head their way.

He saw Tim and John carrying his spare receiving board equipment onto the other boat along with two more monitors.

And then he watched John hop back aboard Mother Earth and help Tina board the smaller vessel.

Bryce looked at the captain, "They are stealing my equipment, Captain!"

"No, Bryce. They will be putting that equipment to good use.

"That boat is not a commercial vessel. It belongs to a friend of Tina's. And, I believe that friend just happens to own some news websites.

"In fact, some of his people will be setting up their equipment here, and I think a few others are heading to your father's office as we speak."

Bryce reached for his phone, but the captain grabbed Bryce's wrist, "Boy, I'm glad you decided to hand me your phone without my having to ask for it."

"You can't do that!" Bryce exclaimed.

"Oh! But I can. I am the captain. You should learn some maritime law. And by the way, those had better *be* shrimp boats."

Just as their exchange ended, the smaller craft pulled away and sped off after Carly.

Aboard the smaller vessel, Tim began setting up the receiving equipment as another crew member was setting up the video gear.

Tina talked with their host who was steering the boat, "Tobias, I adore you! This is the real deal! Are your crews ready to talk to everyone—the senator; his boy, Bryce; and the captain? And are you ready to save the world!"

Tobias was a flamboyant, middle-aged man with way too much money. Smiling from ear to ear, Tobias replied, "Darling, who would've thought that *I* would be the one to out Senator Bolemo. No. I don't mean…Wait. I *do* mean Bolemo—for, at the very least, the *criminal* that he is?"

Tim chuckled at their exchange as he finished setting up the monitoring equipment. At first some of the images were still not clear, so Tina came to Tim's aid and turned a few dials and flipped some switches on the mixing board. Watching Bryce earlier as he had worked on the receiving board had paid off. Crystal clear images were now streaming in on the monitor screen. Hooray! Success!

CHAPTER 18

WORLD WIDE WEB

Speeding ahead, Carly soon caught up with the whales. She came alongside of the Old Whale and Otis as they swam at the head of the pack. Just then her radio sounded; it was her mother.

"Carly, stay with the whales and protect your baby. I am in a boat not far behind you.

"We took Bryce's equipment and are going to relay the images back to Mother Earth.

"My friend Tobias—you remember him—he has an interview crew at the senator's office and a crew on Mother Earth putting all of this on the World Wide Web so everyone can see what the whales are trying to show us.

"So, stay with them and protect them. We will catch up with you shortly."

Carly was too angry to be scared. She simply looked at Otis and let him know of the possible danger and that what they needed to show the world needed to happen *now*.

With a wink and what looked like a smile, Otis dove under the sea along with all of the other whales.

The Mother Earth began receiving the live feed from Carly and Otis, and it was like everyone in the whole world had stopped to watch their favorite television program. Even Bryce was surprised at how well his equipment was working.

The captain asked his radioman to contact the incoming vessel.

The Coast Guard captain asked Captain Adare to slow Mother Earth's speed and prepare to be boarded.

At about that same time, Tobias' crew began broadcasting the live feed from both Carly and Otis throughout all of Tobias' 12 Internet news sites.

Captain Adare replied to the Coast Guard captain, "Sorry, but I cannot do that. You see, we are in the middle of a science experiment being taught by some whales and a young lady."

"What are you talking about?" asked the Coast Guard captain.

Captain Adare explained, "Please go to the Internet. You will see the live feed from the visions of Otis the whale and his friend Carly, and then contact me after you see it."

A few moments later the response came, "That is incredible! Are we actually seeing what they are seeing and thinking?"

"Yes. We have to stay within a certain distance to receive this data, and I will be damned if we will move away. Who sent you?"

The captain of the Coast Guard cutter explained, "We are here at the request of Senator Bolton's office. Why?"

"*Why?*" Captain Adare asked excitedly. "The senator's son is on board here with us, and it seems that the senator didn't want these images publicized.

"Did you happen to notice the commercial vessels near the whale signatures in the Dead Coast zone?"

"We did. We thought that was what this was all about?"

The cameraman signaled to Captain Adare to keep the conversation going.

Captain Adare's reply was an emphatic, "*No!* We believe they are heading out there to harm the whales! And you and I both know that is illegal. You may want to find out what those ships are doing out there and who sent them!"

During the captain's exchange with the Coast Guard, John was talking on the phone with his boss at the university, "I know you were told that this was going to look bad for the school, and I know that you think you have no choice. But right now you just need to go to on the Internet and watch. This is landing-on-the-moon big! You can fire me afterwards." And then John hung up the phone.

Bryce simply stood there feeling a bit ill.

After a few moments the Coast Guard ship turned away from Mother Earth and headed towards the ships that were closing in on the whales.

Captain Adare smiled broadly at Bryce.

While all of this was happening at sea, the second camera crew had reached the senator's office and set up their web link in his foyer.

And it just so happened that at this same instant, the senator walked out of his office talking on his cell phone saying, "It looks like we will be dining on whale tonight."

The senator stopped his tracks as a reporter pointed a microphone at him and asked, "Really, Senator? Why would you say *'dining on whale tonight?'* That is a very odd thing to dine on, don't you think?"

CHAPTER 19

WHAT HEROS DO

The whales dove into depths of the Dead Coast waters, and Tina's suspected horrors came to life. But the horrors beneath the sea were far worse than she had ever imagined. For the first time in the history of the world, Tina, along with all of humanity, could see the world through the eyes of the whales.

As the whales dove deeper, the water changed from clear to murky to black. The crude oil from multiple spills over the decades had accumulated and settled on the sea floor making the water deadly to wildlife.

What was once a vibrant marine ecosystem was no more. Otis showed the world what a lifeless sea floor looks like—thick, blackened water; dried up coral reefs; piles of fish bones; and empty crab shells scattered everywhere.

Otis could not stay long in this toxic environment, needing to frequently return to the surface for air. And with each dive that he made, he showed yet another horrific scene.

The sea was now a poisonous mix of ocean water and chemicals—chemicals that appeared to emanate from the shoreline. The chemicals turned the water to an ugly neon green just above the oil-soaked bottom, rendering this level to be also devoid of life.

The next level up seemed to have a tiny bit of life, but only because an occasional school of fish would zip through this area. However, it was evident that any life found within this level was surely struggling to survive. One fish even died in front of Otis while the whole world watched it gasping as it tried desperately to get oxygen from the contaminated water.

The uppermost level of the sea was slightly different because there were still a few small signs of life there.

And finally, covering the water's surface were huge algae blooms sucking oxygen from the water and blocking the sunlight from reaching the deeper depths of the sea.

Seeing the desolation within each level made the images on the monitor screens look like an incredibly frightening, never-ending horror movie.

Next the camera turned to John who explained what was happening at each level and how this area had not been like this just 10 years before.

He explained how thousands of nautical miles of sea had been turned into dead zones throughout the world and that this place was one of the *smaller* areas.

He explained how pollution was causing the oceans to die and the effect that this was having on all wildlife worldwide.

John's closing statement was clear: "This *is* actually happening now. This is not fake news or some sort of deception. This is a *genuine* problem that is growing exponentially.

"The water here can no longer diffuse the pollution, and as a result, has succumbed to it. That is why this area is known as the Dead Coast.

"Do you understand that if the oceans die, we *all* die—not just marine life, not just humans, but *every* living thing on the *entire* planet?

"*We* are our own life-ending event, not some asteroid from space. By the way, we funded the research to take care of asteroids, but we did nothing to clean up *this*, and *this* is happening right here! Right now!

"This problem is *immense!* And humanity's disregard in taking care of our planet—our home—is beyond comprehension. The problem is so immense that the whales had to tell us about the problem. Hell! They had to *show* us! *Now will you listen!*"

While John gave his talk, the "shrimp boats" were closing in on Carly. And the other camera crew was closing in on Bryce's father, Senator Bolton.

At the senator's office, the camera crew would not let Senator Bolton—or "Bolemo" as he was called—back away from the camera. One person even blocked the office door.

When the reporter started asking questions, the senator's only reply was "No comment." And acting like a cornered rat, the senator scampered around his office trying to escape the reporter's questioning.

The reporter asked, "Senator, as you know, Dr. John Gardner from the University of Miami just explained what the whales have been trying to show us for many decades—that the pollution coming from the companies of many of *your* financial backers is to blame? Do you have any comment?"

"Finally!" Bolton thought. He could finally get a word in. He was ready to comment now because he was so practiced at dodging this question—he had been dodging it for decades all the while destroying the environment by voting against regulations for pollution control, defunding the EPA, voting to pull out of the Paris accord, and blocking research.

The senator stopped and glared at the reporter. He straightened his American-flag necktie and started to answer the reporter's question.

But this reporter was no novice. He was not about to give the senator an opportunity to spew his typical political rhetoric to deflect the questions. No.

Instead, this reporter just stopped the senator before he could respond, "Senator, never mind. We all know the answer to that. You are just a bought-and-paid-for politician who is owned by lobbyists. You are not a representative of the people who elected you. Instead, you are a representative of those who *fund* you. You're a fraud. And, well, that American-flag necktie does not belong on you!"

The senator was trapped. He knew he had played right into the reporter's hands.

The reporter continued, "By the way, Senator, what *did* you mean when you said, 'We will be dining on whale tonight'?

"Because, as you know, this is a worldwide, live broadcast on the Internet with about 500 million viewers watching right now. And it has been confirmed that you requested that the Coast Guard intercept the research vessel Mother Earth while several other non-Coast Guard vessels are heading towards Carly and the whale Otis.

"Tell the world, Senator, why you would make a statement like that, and why are those ships now heading to that location?"

For once, the senator was speechless; however, his assistant stepped up and made a statement.

She grabbed the microphone, "Hello. I'm Janice. And it is time for my 15 minutes of fame.

Here you go, Mr. Reporter. Here is the email he sent to one of his biggest contributors yesterday."

The reporter turned the paper to the camera and read it aloud for the senator and everyone to hear:

> *Look. It is a small problem. Don't worry about this whale business.*
>
> *My son is on board that ship and will sabotage any attempts to broadcast the polluted water or this stupid whale tale.*
>
> *If he fails, but he won't, I have a backup plan for this.*
>
> *You have a few ships at your disposal. Send them out and at least harpoon the smallest whale. Just kill him off, and this all goes away for good.*
>
> *If you do this, I can guarantee a "Yes" vote for you to pay no corporate tax on that operation you had in the gulf.*

Then the reporter added, "And you call yourself an American. Shameful.

"To the captain of the Mother Earth, *those whales are in extreme danger!*"

CHAPTER 20

THE RACE IS ON

The message came through loud and clear not only to Captain Adare and Tina, but also to the captain of the Coast Guard cutter. The cutter made an abrupt turn and headed off at full speed toward Carly and Otis.

Tina immediately radioed the captain, "Dear, I'm trying to reach Carly."

While all of this played out on the World Wide Web, Carly was completely shocked by the destruction she was witnessing from Otis' visions. Knowing how the sea was dying and that the rest of the earth would soon follow, she wept openly until the squelch of her radio interrupted her thoughts.

"Carly! Where is Otis? Do you see those other ships yet? Those ships are on the way to kill Otis!" Tina warned.

Carly fumbled with the buttons and responded, "I see them! They're not far from Otis! I have to go!" Then Tina's radio went silent.

Tina looked at Tobias helplessly. Tobias winked and said, "Don't worry, Darling, we can go way faster than this.

"*Now, boys! Gun it!*"

The boat lurched forward and started skipping across the waves at break-neck speed.

Just as Tobias' boat was nearing Carly, Carly realized that she was closing in on the ship closest to Otis. She concentrated on Otis and told him over and over, "Stay under the water, Otis! Stay under the water! Do not surface!"

Carly started getting feelings from Otis; he was gasping for air. Her little launch was at full speed, and soon she closed in on the boat that was the size of a shrimp boat. But this was no shrimp boat.

On the bow of this boat stood a huge man holding a harpoon gun, steadily sweeping it back and forth as he watched for Otis to come up for air.

Suddenly, Carly felt Otis' need to surface now because he was out of air.

Even with all of her fear, Carly had an advantage over the larger boat: She knew where Otis was going to surface and immediately headed in that direction.

Just as Otis was coming to the surface on the port side of the ship, a watcher yelled, "Thar she blows!"

The burly man turned the massive harpoon gun onto his target, Otis, and pulled the trigger. And with a loud boom, the harpoon gun launched its deadly six-foot spear.

As the spear soared toward the baby whale, a small boat intercepted its path just a second before it reached its target. With a thunderous crash, the spear ripped through the hull of Carly's boat, throwing

Carly out of her shattered launch and into the warm waters of the Gulf.

Otis witnessed this and watched as the small boat burst into flames. He franticly looked for Carly, diving and rising several times and finally spotting her swimming towards him. He gently swam beside her, and she climbed onto his back and tightly held onto him. Through their shared visions, this entire exchange was broadcast live to nearly a billion people across the World Wide Web.

While Otis was retrieving Carly from the water, the killer ship had been maneuvered into position for a second shot at Otis. But just as it had gotten into place, something suddenly jolted it, and then again, and then jolted it again!

The other whales were slamming themselves into the hulls of not only that ship, but also into the hulls of the other four ships that were also closing in on Carly and Otis! The 80-ton behemoths of the ocean repeatedly slammed into the sides of these vessels.

Carly stood on Otis' back and watched as the whales pummeled the ships. Then she began cheering. She knew now that they were going to live and that the whole world now knew the truth, too.

As Carly screamed at the ships and cheered for the whales, Tobias' boat pulled alongside them. Tina dove into the water and swam to Carly and Otis. She climbed onto Otis' back and began cheering as well.

A short time later, the Coast Guard cutter was positioned next to the killer boats. The Coast Guard captain pointed his ship's cannons at the other vessels and ordered them to stand down. When the other boats powered down, the whales stopped beating the boats' hulls.

CHAPTER 21

REPERCUSSIONS

As the Coast Guard was rounding up the other ships, Captain Adare picked up the microphone, stepped in front of the camera, and pulled Bryce beside him.

"People of the world, you now see what our world is facing. You now know firsthand that our death is coming just as surely as the senator and his corporate cronies tried to kill Carly and Otis.

"This is no hoax. This is real, folks. And we not only have the bravery of Carly and a baby right whale named Otis to thank, but also the senator's own son, Bryce Bolton.

"Bryce did his best to expose the corporate greed that led to the immeasurable degree of pollution that is causing the death of the earth.

"We owe all of them our gratitude, and we owe it *to* all of them to reverse the course of our demise. We all can pitch in to save the world just as Carly and Otis did today."

Bryce stood there with a blank look on his face.

While Captain Adare was broadcasting, Tobias called to Tina and Carly, "Ladies! We are still on the air. Is there anything you would like to say?"

Carly let go of her mother and lay down on Otis' back with her head near his eye. The camera panned down to them, and Carly began, "My baby and I have showed you the direction in which this planet is heading. And now, because of everyone else involved, you know how it got this way.

"Money is not worth the life of even *one* creature on this planet. We share this world with every*thing*, not just everyone. We owe it to ourselves and to each other to understand this.

"Otis and I will keep fighting. But you need to do your part, too. This does not end here. This is only the beginning.

"And you, Senator Bolemo, or whatever your name is, you, sir, will pay dearly for trying to kill my baby and me. This fight is not over. The earth will win!"

The camera panned across the water to show Coast Guardsmen boarding the killer ships.

Shortly after that, the news crew at Senator Bolton's office watched the police stream into the office and handcuff the senator despite all of his protests.

Then the website went blank, but not before the whole world had become profoundly moved by the events that had taken place before everyone's eyes.

It was because Otis, the Old Whale, and all whales possess the inherent knowledge of the end of the world plus their perseverance in trying to communicate this knowledge to humanity for hundreds of years along with the bravery of a young girl and her friends that saving the earth became possible today.

CHAPTER 22

TOGETHER AGAIN

Having completed their mission of revealing the death and destruction in the area of the Gulf known as the Dead Coast and exposing the corruption that contributed to this atrocity and others like it around the world, Carly, Otis, Tina, and Tobias returned to the Mother Earth.

Everyone was together again—Carly, John, Tim, Captain Adare, Ellie, Tina, and now Tobias.

Bryce had already left the ship. He knew he was as guilty and as complicit as his criminal father.

Otis swam beside Mother Earth spouting water every now and again joining in the revelry with his friends who were celebrating on the bow of the ship.

Ellie was the first to address everyone, "Why did no one tell me what was going on?"

John looked at her, "Honey, you have moments of being Eleanor every now and again, and you have a reputation that we did not want to damage.

As long as you did not know what was going on, and if we had been wrong, then you could at least return to your life as Eleanor. But we are all very glad that you are *our* Ellie."

The captain raised his glass in a salute to the crew and to Otis and said, "Great job, everyone!

"Carly, I am proud of you and Otis. And I am proud of the other whales as well. We still have much work to do. We have a world to keep saving."

As the sun set and Mother Earth sailed along, the great Old Whale breached the ocean's surface just ahead of the ship, and a giant wave soaked the jovial crew. And according to Carly and Otis, it was the Old Whale's way of thanking them.

ಹಿ ✳ ಆ

We are not alone in this universe, not because of space aliens, but because of our neighbors that already share planet earth with us—on the land, in the sea, and in the air.

ಹಿ ✳ ಆ

THE END

ABOUT THE AUTHOR

Matthew Beggarly was born in 1970 to Dan and Gloria Beggarly of Baltimore, Maryland. When he was nine years old, Matt and his family moved from the big city to the small town of BelAir, Maryland.

Then just two years later, a life-altering event occurred that would shape the rest of Matt's life—his mother was taken by cancer, and his family structure was understandably shaken. Matt went on to graduate from BelAir Senior High School and then attended Harford Community College.

However, through his mid-20s and into his early 30s, Matt struggled with alcoholism and addiction, which ultimately ended his marriage along with a prominent career as an insurance broker. During this time, though, he was blessed with a beautiful baby daughter, Lindsay, whom he loves dearly.

As the years passed, careers had come and gone, and then at the age of 42, just one week after his 25-

year high school class reunion, as Matt was dining in a restaurant, he suddenly suffered a life-ending heart attack—the kind known as a widow maker because it is so severe that only four people per year ever survive it. And by the grace of God, Matt was resuscitated by a quick-acting restaurant employee who performed live-saving CPR until the emergency medical team arrived.

Matt underwent a triple-bypass heart surgery as well as the implantation of five additional stents. Unfortunately, during this heart surgery, he suffered a stroke, which caused the left side of his body to become severely weakened.

Matt was undaunted by his situation, and he had a strong desire to live. His family took him in and cared for him through his recovery. It was during this time that he decided to return to a childhood passion that he had shared with his mother—writing, so he started keeping a journal.

After a few years of self-rehabilitation, a bout with non-Hodgkin's Lymphoma, and a small audio-nerve brain tumor, both of which are now in remission, Matt was able to do something he had never done before. He went on to compete in a sprint triathlon in the spring of 2016, and then he followed that with four more events that summer.

Then, in addition to his other medical conditions, Matt was diagnosed with medically-related PTSD.

One day a friend said, "You can die living or live dying," and that struck a chord with Matt.

With this saying stuck in his head and his experience of dying one time already, Matt did not want to die again leaving behind damaged relationships and unfulfilled dreams.

In September of 2016, Matt followed one of his dreams and began his journey as the first stroke survivor to ever bicycle solo across the United States.

It was a journey like no other. Even though he had no long-distance bicycling experience, and despite being the victim of a hit-and-run accident on his first day on the road, Matt continued to pedal his 50-dollar bicycle across the country.

It was during this ride that Matt took to online blogging and found himself truly enjoying sharing his experiences and bringing hope to the thousands who followed his journal that they, too, could still do something epic in their own lives. Sadly though, that initial journey abruptly ended when, while riding his bike outside of Dallas, Texas, Matt was struck by a truck.

Before starting this adventure in 2016, Matt had moved from Maryland to Jacksonville, Florida, the place from where he had planned to begin his cross-country journey, so he returned to Jacksonville to recover from this latest accident.

While recuperating, Matt undertook a writing assignment that placed him aboard a small yacht that was traveling The Great Loop of North America.

On the beautiful waterways of America, Matt discovered the joy of writing about his experiences along with other stories that he had been hoping to tell. And it was during a swim with a pod of wild dolphins in the waters of the Intracoastal Waterway that the story of Carly & Otis was born.

After sailing for only a few months, Matt had to leave the ship early due to some unforeseen circumstances back home, so he returned to Jacksonville once again where he finished this amazing tale; began mentoring young, at-risk teens with the juvenile justice department in Florida; and truly became not only a survivor, but a tri-athlete, a sponsored athlete, and now a published author...all after dying one day.

With many of his other dreams now fulfilled, in the fall of 2017 Matt decided to finish the journey that he had started the year before. But before doing so, he had to put to rest a resurgence of the non-Hodgkin's Lymphoma. And, thankfully, it appears to be at rest again.

And so, as of this writing, Matt is bicycling across the country writing his tales, following his dreams, and living a life of adventure that most people only dream about—inspiring people by leaving the herd behind and forging his own path through life in this great, big, beautiful world.

This story is a work of fiction.
All of the events and characters are fictitious,
and any resemblance to actual events or persons, living or dead,
is purely coincidental.

63093280R00080

Made in the USA
Middletown, DE
29 January 2018